# THE GUNSMITH

# 487

## Tales of a Swamper

# THE GUNSMITH

# 487

## Tales of a Swamper

J.R. Roberts

SPEAKING VOLUMES, LLC
NAPLES, FLORIDA
2023

Tales of a Swamper

Copyright © 2023 by Robert J. Randisi

ISBN 979-8-89022-098-1

# Chapter One

Firecreek, Wyoming

Clint Adams took an entirely new outlook on his visit to Firecreek, Wyoming. His normal approach was to board his horse, Toby, in the nearest livery to the hotel he chose. When he checked in, he usually did it under his own name and let the chips fall where they may.

This time he decided to check in under a different name and see just how much rest he could get before somebody recognized him.

"Here you go, Mr. McCord," the clerk said, handing him his key. "And enjoy your stay in our quiet little town."

"Thank you," Clint said. "I will."

He had signed the register John McCord from Dallas. There was no reason for anyone to believe differently.

He chose a hotel with a dining room, so he took his rifle and saddlebags to his room first and then went to have a meal.

It wasn't just the clerk's word that Firecreek was a quiet town. It felt quiet as he rode in, and now, as he sat in a mostly empty dining room, it still felt that way. This was why he chose to register under an assumed name, because he wanted the town to stay quiet.

Before leaving his room, he considered leaving his gun behind. But ultimately, he disregarded such a thought. There was always the chance he might be recognized, and without his gun he would be a sitting duck.

He finished his first meal in town, and then went out to the hotel's front porch. There was very little activity on the street, but he decided to pull up a chair, sit in front of the hotel, and watch. No, rather than just watch, he was going to observe.

Of late he had been rereading Edgar Allan Poe's tales of "ratiocination." These were "*Murder in the Rue Morgue,*" "*The Mystery of Marie Roget,*" and "*The Purloined Letter.*" Rereading these first detective tales of C. Auguste Dupin had made him curious about observing life rather than just watching it go by.

At first he thought to sit in a wicker chair in front of the hotel and read these tales, but in the end he decided to just sit and observe.

***

Harry Hayes finished swamping out the Jack of Spades Saloon in time for the bartender, Race Gentry, to open the front doors and kick him out.

"And get this done earlier tomorrow," Gentry yelled, "or I'll get somebody else."

"Hey," Hayes shouted, "my money."

Gentry fished four bits out of his pocket and tossed it into the street.

Two men passing by watched this interaction and one asked, "You open yet, Race?"

"I am," Gentry said, heartily, "come in, come in."

Harry Hayes picked his four bits out of the dirt, cleaned the coins off and put them in his pocket. Then he moved on to his next job, swamping out a nearby livery stable.

He turned, looked across the street and locked eyes with a man seated in front of the Campfire Hotel, exchanged a wave, and moved on.

\*\*\*

Clint watched as a man who was probably the bartender at the Jack of Spades Saloon, tossed a man into the street. He assumed the man was the saloon swamper, for the bartender tossed some money into the street and shouted at him to come in earlier, the next day. The man picked his coins up off the street, turned and gave Clint a short wave—which he saw no harm in returning—and moved on down the street.

Clint had camped only two miles outside of town the night before. As a result, he had ridden in early and checked into his hotel before the town could wake up. As a result, he had taken up a position in front of the hotel in time to observe it awakening.

People began to appear on the streets, shops were opening—a General Store, Leather Works and Dress Shop within easy view. The only one of interest at the moment was the Dress Shop, where a lovely young woman unlocked the front door and entered. Moments later, the CLOSED sign was turned to the OPEN side.

The man who opened the General Store looked like a typical storekeeper, with a white apron covering him from neck to ankles.

A big beefy man opened the Leather Works shop, looking for all the world like he wished he was some-where else.

As Clint continued to observe, the old man who had been tossed from the saloon walked down to the liv-ery—the same livery he had left his Tobiano—and en-tered. He would probably be in there a while, cleaning out stalls.

And as the town continued to wake, Clint found himself with plenty of activity to entertain him.

# Chapter Two

Clint found this business of observing to be very restful. And while he was sitting there, no one gave the slightest inkling of recognizing him. It would probably be easier for someone to identify him in a saloon, rather than seated in front of a hotel. In fact, several people had graced him with a nod as they passed him, which he returned, but no one stared.

Clint continued to relax in his chair until his stomach told him it was lunch time. Lunch was something that fell by the wayside when you were on the trail. He rose to breakfast, and ate supper before turning in. But when he was in a town, lunch fell nicely into place.

He stood up from his chair, and chose a direction to walk, in search of a likely café.

\*\*\*

Harry Hayes finished sweeping out the empty horse stalls in the livery, collected his money from the owner, and left.

As he headed for his next job, he saw, coming toward him, the man who had been sitting in front of the hotel.

"You look lost, friend," he said.

"I'm looking for a place to have lunch."

"I suggest Caroline's Café, two more streets in this direction," Hayes said, jerking his thumb.

"Good food?"

"For lunch, yeah," Hayes said, "for supper, no."

"Thanks for the tip," Clint said.

"You need anything else, ask for Harry Hayes," the man told him.

"John McCord."

"Yeah, okay," Hayes said.

As Clint continued on, Hayes wondered why the Gunsmith was staying in town under an assumed name.

\*\*\*

Clint found Caroline's, went in, and easily found an isolated table since the place was pretty empty.

The waiter took Clint's order for a turkey sandwich and brought it out quickly.

"Somebody recommend us?" the waiter asked.

"Yes, a fella named Harry Hayes."

"The swamper," the waiter said.

"That's what they call him, the Swamper."

"Oh, I get it. Does he clean here, as well?"

"Yup, in the evening after we close."

Clint decided not to tell the man what Harry Hayes said about Caroline's, and bit into his sandwich. It was pretty good, and he washed it down with a sip of coffee that was too weak.

\*\*\*

Harry Hayes stopped into the hotel "McCord" was staying in and asked the desk clerk some questions. Since the clerk knew how nosy Harry was, he answered his questions.

"John McCord from Dallas," he told the swamper.

"How long's he stayin'?" Harry asked.

"Dunno," the clerk said, "he didn't say."

"Okay, Leroy, thanks."

Leroy watched as Harry walked out. He was aware the swamper knew more about the people in town than anybody else. While he cleaned, he watched and listened. That included when he came in at night and cleaned the lobby floor of the Campfire Hotel.

\*\*\*

When Clint came out of Caroline's, he pretty much approved of it for lunch. The food was edible, but he wished he had asked Harry Hayes for the name of a place for supper. Oh well, he figured he would be able to find the old timer and ask.

He walked back to his hotel, once again exchanging a nod or two of greeting with the passing citizens. When he reached the hotel, his chair was empty, so he once again occupied it and figured to do so until he got hungry for supper.

\*\*\*

While Harry Hayes was sweeping out the sheriff's office, he was tempted to tell Sheriff Harlow that Clint Adams was in town under the name John McCord. But in the end, he decided not to. The man must have a reason for it.

Harlow looked up from the wanted posters and asked, "Anythin' new in town, Harry?"

"Not that I know of Sheriff."

"Nobody new in town?"

"Well . . ."

"Come on, old timer, give," Harlow snapped at him.

"Over at the Campfire a new fella checked in."

"What's his name?"

"McCord, John McCord."

Harlow looked down at the posters in his hands.

"Don't have anythin' for somebody by that name. What's he like?"

"He likes sittin' out in front of the hotel."

"He just sits there?"

"Yessir."

"Doin' what?"

"Nothin'," Hayes said. "He just . . . watches."

"Well," Harlow said, "I guess I'll check him out, but there's no hurry, if all he's doin' is watchin'."

"Yessir," Hayes said. He finished his sweeping and moved on.

# Chapter Three

Clint watched as citizens of all ages and sizes traversed the streets of Firecreek. By afternoon, the children began flooding the streets, probably after school. The ladies seemed to come out in the late afternoon, many of them shopping in the General Store, probably for the makings of supper for their families.

At one point Harry Hayes put in another appearance, apparently on his way to another swamper job. As he walked past, he waved to Clint, who beckoned him over.

"You seem to be a pretty busy man," Clint said.

"Gotta make a livin'," Hayes said. "How was your lunch?"

"Edible," Clint said. "What do you recommend for supper?"

"Ah, somethin' more than edible," Hayes said. "The Cattleman Steak House—" he pointed, "three streets that way." The direction was the opposite from Caroline's.

"It's not a private club for cattlemen?" Clint asked.

"Naw," Hayes said, "it's just a name. Anybody can go in and eat."

"And I assume steak is their specialty?"

Hayes smiled and said, "Real special."

"Well, thanks again," Clint said. "And while I have you here, is this hotel a good place to have breakfast?"

"As good as any," Hayes said.

"Thanks again."

Hayes stared at Clint for a few moments before moving on. Clint knew the look. Harry Hayes recognized him but didn't say a word. It remained to be seen if the situation would stay that way.

He watched Hayes walk away, then decided to go inside and ask some questions.

"Can I help you, Sir?" the desk clerk asked. He looked to be in his mid-thirties, very thin with a wide space between his two front teeth.

"What's your name?"

"Leroy, Sir."

"Do you know a fella named Harry Hayes?"

"Yes, Sir," Leroy said. "He's the town swamper."

"I've heard of a saloon swamper," Clint said, "but a town swamper?"

"He cleans out most of the places in town."

"Does that include the sheriff's office?"

"Oh, yes, Sir. But his biggest job is the Jack of Spades Saloon."

"I saw him get thrown out of that place this morning," Clint said.

"That's probably true, but they'll let him in late tonight to clean up. Have you had some trouble with Harry?"

"Not at all," Clint said. "In fact, he's suggested some places for me to eat—including this one for breakfast."

"We do have a good breakfast, here," Leroy said.

"I'll sample it tomorrow morning," Clint said. "Right now I'm going to the Cattleman Steak House for supper."

"Best place in town," Leroy said.

"That's what Harry said," Clint replied. "Thanks for confirming it."

"My pleasure, Sir."

Clint went back outside. It was still a little early for supper, so he stuck his butt back in the chair.

***

Harry Hayes hurried away from the Campfire Hotel. He had other jobs too. Then he would allow himself some rest before the big job of cleaning out the Jack of Spades Saloon.

But he also rushed away because he had almost blurted out the Gunsmith's name, when he suddenly realized he could put the man's presence in town to good use.

He just wasn't sure what that use would be . . . yet.

\*\*\*

Clint gave it another hour, then rose and began walking in the direction Harry Hayes had told him the Cattleman's Steak House was.

"Cattleman" was a popular name for many clubs and restaurants in many towns. When he came to this one, he noticed it was not as opulent as the others he had been to. He only hoped the steaks lived up to the name.

He presented himself at the door and was shown to a table against a side wall. Luckily, when he was dining alone, he usually got a table by a wall, since a fourth chair was not necessary. Tables in the center of the room were occupied by mostly families of four.

"Welcome, Sir," the waiter in a dark suit greeted him. "You're new in town?"

"Yes, I am," Clint said. "Your restaurant was recommended to me as a place for an excellent steak."

"Whoever made the suggestion did not steer you wrong," the man said. "All the trimmings?"

Clint smiled.

"As much as I can get," he said.

"You won't be disappointed, Sir," the waiter said. "A mug of cold beer while you wait?"

"That sounds fine," Clint said, "just fine."

# Chapter Four

As promised by Harry Hayes, the steak was excellent, as was the pie that followed.

"How was your meal, Sir?" the waiter asked.

"Very good," Clint said. "I'll be coming back, again."

"We look forward to it."

The waiter walked Clint to the door.

"One question," Clint said.

"Yes?"

"Does the sheriff ever eat here?"

"I'm afraid the prices are a little beyond the reach of his salary," the waiter said.

"I see," Clint said. "Thank you."

Clint had no desire to run into the local law, on the off chance the man might recognize him. But his desire didn't matter, because as he entered the lobby of his hotel, he saw a man there, wearing a badge.

"Mr. McCord?" he asked.

"That's right."

"I'm Sheriff Harlow," the man said.

"What can I do for you, Sheriff?"

"I just like to check in with strangers," the lawman said, "and find out why they're in town, and for how long?"

"Well, I'm just passing through, really," Clint said, "but I've found it to be a nice, quiet place to rest, so I may be staying for a few days."

"Okay, then," Harlow said, "enjoy yourself. I just ask that you stay out of trouble."

"Trouble is something I never look for, Sheriff."

"That's good to hear, Mr. McCord," Harlow said. "Have a good evenin'."

As Harlow walked away, Clint went through the lobby to the stairs and up to his room.

Clint read Poe until late hours of the night and then turned in.

\*\*\*

Harry Hayes got busy cleaning the Jack of Spades Saloon, starting in the back, while Race Gentry was getting the large front room cleared out for the night.

About half-an-hour later, Hayes heard the front door open to admit a man named Victor King. The old man stood at the door to listen to their conversation, occasionally sweeping his broom across the floor so it could be heard.

They were planning something. Harry couldn't always hear every word, but enough to know it was illegal. He collected lots of bits and pieces from all the jobs he had. When he put them together, he knew what was going on all over town.

One of these days he'd figure out what to do with all this information.

\*\*\*

Clint had an early breakfast in his hotel and was out front in his chair in time to see Harry Hayes get kicked out of the saloon. When the old man had gotten to his feet and picked his pay up from the street, he turned and waved at Clint. Clint returned the wave, then beckoned him over.

"How about a cup of coffee, Harry?" he asked.

"I wouldn't mind," the old man said.

"Wait here, I'll go in and get it."

Clint went inside and came out with two steaming cups. He sat in his chair and Harry sat on the edge of the boardwalk.

"Whataya been seein', sittin' in this chair?" Harry asked.

"Well, I've been seeing you, Harry."

"Me? Whataya seein' me doin'? My job?"

16

"You do your job in lots of places," Clint said. "And I think you're keeping your ears open."

"Why would I do that?"

"Because you go in and out of places and nobody notices you," Clint said. "I'll bet you know all the secrets in town."

"Well, I know one secret," Hayes said.

"And what's that?"

He looked around to make sure nobody could hear him, then looked at Clint and said, "You're Clint Adams."

"And how do you know that?" Clint asked, not bothering to deny it.

"I seen you once in Wichita," Hayes said.

Clint had been to Wichita several times and knew what he was doing each time.

"And what were you doing in Wichita?" he asked.

"Same thing I'm doin' here," Hayes said, "only I was younger."

Clint studied Hayes' face but couldn't place it. If he was swamping out places in Wichita, Clint never noticed him.

"And what did you do with your secrets from Wichita?" Clint asked.

"Nothin'," Harry said. "I was too young and wasn't smart enough to know what I had."

"And you know what you have here?"

"Pretty much."

"Do you intend to tell the sheriff?"

"Hell, no," Hayes said. "He wouldn't do nothin'. I'm just gonna keep it to myself for a while." Hayes stood up and handed the empty cup back to Clint. "Thanks for the coffee . . . Mr. McCord."

# Chapter Five

Clint spent the next few days with his butt firmly planted in his wicker chair, watching the town go by. He enjoyed watching the pretty young woman open her dress shop each day, and watching Harry Hayes go from job to job with his broom. He noticed one of the old man's stops was the Freight and Stage office. Keeping his ears open in that place could lead to much useful information.

On occasion the sheriff would walk by and give Clint a nod, which he returned.

He took his meals each day in the same places—breakfast at his hotel, lunch at the café and supper at the steak house. The waiters in each place were getting to know him.

To this point he had not yet entered the Jack of Spades Saloon, but on this day, he decided to quit his chair for a while and have a beer. He stood up and crossed to the saloon.

***

Race Gentry had noticed the man seated in front of the hotel on the second day. Now, two days later, the man was still there. What was he doing? What the hell was he watching?

When he saw the man enter the saloon, he was surprised. After days of sitting and watching, what made him come in?

"Finally decided to come in, eh?" he asked, as the man reached the bar.

"I got thirsty," the man said. "How about a beer?"

"Comin' up."

***

Clint saw the bartender watching him as he approached. He wondered how long it would take for him to ask. The saloon was large, with gaming tables and girls. At this time of the afternoon, it was half full.

The bartender put a beer in front of him and waited while he drank half of it down.

"What've you been sittin' out there watching for?" Gentry asked him.

"Nothing," Clint said. "I'm just . . . watching."

"What's your name?"

"McCord. What's yours?"

"I'm Race Gentry," the man said. "How long do you intend to sit there watchin'?"

"I don't know," Clint said. "I have no plan beyond watching and eating."

"And now drinkin'," Gentry said.

"Yes," Clint said, "and drinking, occasionally." He finished his beer.

"Another?" Gentry asked.

"No. I said I'll drink occasionally. Maybe later."

"Well, come back when you're ready," Gentry said. "To drink, maybe to gamble, or maybe for a girl."

"I'll consider all that," Clint promised, and left the saloon. He crossed the street and sat back down in his chair.

***

After Clint left the saloon, another man came up to the bar.

"Who is he?" he asked Gentry.

"He says his name is McCord."

"What's he here for?"

"He says just to watch."

"But who's he watchin'?" the man asked. "Us?"

"Why else would he be sitting right across the street?"

"I don't know," Gentry said.

"Well, we can't make a move while we're bein' watched," the other man said.

"I know, Teach, I know," Gentry said. "So we're gonna find out why he's here."

"How?" Teach asked.

"Give me some time to think," Gentry said. "Have another beer."

\*\*\*

Clint watched as more men went into the saloon than came out as the day wore on. The lights from within shone out the door and the windows, along with music and laughter. And from down the street came the swamper, Harry Hayes, to stand beside Clint.

"It's in full swing," the old man said. "I'll have plenty to clean in the morning."

"It looks like you will."

Hayes looked at Clint.

"Are you gonna go inside?"

"I've been inside," Clint answered.

"And met Gentry, the bartender?"

"I met him."

"He's also the owner," Hayes said. "And he has other plans."

"Plans that you know of?"

"Plans I've overheard some of," Hayes said. "I'm still waiting to learn it all."

"And whose plans have you also heard from the other places you clean?" Clint asked.

"I know of a plan or two."

"You haven't told anyone who I am, have you?" Clint asked.

"I ain't told nobody nothin', Mr. McCord."

Clint believed the older man.

# Chapter Six

Hayes drifted away to get some sleep, or do another job, Clint didn't know which. The activity across the street was going to go on for some time, and it was getting too dark to see much of anything. Clint stood up, preparing to go inside, when he saw something odd. The front door of the dress shop opened and the young lady who owned it stepped outside. He watched as she locked the door, started to turn to go inside the hotel when he saw two men come from the dark and grab her. He stepped into the street and hurried over, wondering if one of the men was a husband or boyfriend.

". . . told you to leave me alone, Larry."

"Well, I ain't through with you yet, Holly."

"I'm through with *you*," she said, forcefully.

The other man laughed.

"You're hurting my arm!" she snapped.

"You heard the lady," Clint said, stepping up onto the boardwalk.

All three of the people in front of the door turned to look at him.

"This ain't none of your business, Mister," Larry said.

"If the lady needs help, I'm making it my business."

Up close Clint could see both men were in their early thirties. The girl looked to be in her late twenties.

"This fella's lookin' fer trouble, Larry," the other man said.

"He sure is, Caleb," Larry said, then turned his attention back to Clint. "This here's my woman, friend."

"I am no such thing!" the girl snapped.

"You heard the lady," Clint said. "Now let her go or there's going to be trouble."

"And just who're you to threaten us?" Caleb asked.

"I'm the man who's going to make sure you're sorry you ever met me, that's who," Clint said. "Now let her go."

Larry thought a moment, then released the girl's arm and said, to his friend, "Let's go, Caleb."

Caleb hesitated, but Larry pushed him, and the two men walked away.

"Are you all right, Miss?" Clint asked.

"I'm fine, thank you."

"Was that man your fella?"

"Once, maybe," she said, "until I realized what he was really like."

"Do you live far from here?"

"It's a few blocks walk," she said.

"Would you allow me to walk you home?"

"If you'll call me Holly."

"That's fine," he said, "and you can call me John."

"All right, John, let's walk this way."

They started away from the store.

"I've noticed you sitting in front of the hotel these past few days," she said. "Are you waiting for someone?"

"Nope."

"Watching someone?"

"Everyone."

"What for?"

He shrugged.

"Just to watch."

"Waiting for a lady in distress, perhaps?"

"Always."

"You like saving ladies?"

"I do, yes."

"And do you expect payment?" she asked.

"No, I don't," Clint said.

"Then why do you do it?"

"I help ladies who need help," Clint said.

She stopped walking.

"This is me."

"A hardware store?"

"I live above it. The stairs are in the alley."

"I'll walk you that far, just in case."

They walked into the darkened alley to the stairs.

"This is as far as you go," she said, at the base of the stairs. "No reward, I'm afraid. Except for this." She kissed his cheek.

He smiled.

"That'll do it . . . for now."

"Good night, John."

"Good night, Holly."

He watched her walk up and waited until she went inside. A kiss on the cheek from a lovely young woman was a good way to end a day. He left the alley and walked back to his hotel.

***

Clint got into bed with some Edgar Allan Poe, but Harry Hayes kept getting in the way. He wondered how many people's secrets the old man knew in Firecreek? Upon his arrival in town, Clint's intention was to rest and not get involved in anyone's business. However, after several days of just sitting and watching, he was finding himself interested in whatever Harry Hayes knew.

He was also interested in how long Hayes would keep Clint's identity to himself.

# Chapter Seven

Clint decided he didn't know Harry Hayes well enough to trust him to keep his name a secret. If it suited him, and would do him some good, he felt the old man would give him away. So today, instead of just sitting and watching, he was going to find Harry Hayes and find out what was on his mind.

He started with breakfast in the hotel before stepping out to the front porch of the hotel. He could see that the Jack of Spades Saloon had not yet opened, so he assumed Harry Hayes was still inside.

He had decided to brace Harry when he came out, to find out what was going on behind the scenes of this quiet little town. He had to admit his curiosity was getting the best of him. Sitting and watching was becoming too much of a bore and reading Poe filled only so many nighttime hours. It was time to ask questions.

Harry Hayes came stumbling out of the Jack of Spades, picked up his money from the street, and turned to wave at Clint, who beckoned him over.

"Let's have breakfast, Harry," Clint said.

"On you?"

"On me."

"Lead the way."

Instead of going to the café, Clint decided to take the swamper into the hotel for breakfast. Their meeting would not be so obvious there.

The small dining room was empty, so a corner table was no problem.

After they had both ordered—the waiter giving Harry Hayes a mighty scowl—Harry asked, "What's this about? You tired of watchin'?"

"Does it show?"

Harry cackled.

"You ain't the kinda man who can just sit and watch for very long."

"You still haven't told anyone about me?"

"Not a soul."

"Why not?"

"Tain't nobody's business."

"Why do I think you know everybody's business in town?" Clint asked.

Harry cackled again.

"Now, that's my business," he said.

The waiter came and set a plate of ham-and-eggs in front of each of them.

"And what do you intend to do with all this knowledge?" Clint asked.

"I'm hearin' lots of talk," Harry said. "I guess I'll have to figure out what to do when folks stop talkin' and start doin'."

"And how close is that to happening?"

Harry cackled again and said, "Pretty damn close."

"Is any of it something you want to talk about?"

"Why does that matter to you?"

"Like you said," Clint answered, "I'm getting tired of just watching. I have to admit I'm not just the watching type. So, I've got two choices. One, saddle up and ride out. Two, find out what's going on and deal myself in."

"So yer just lookin' to be nosy."

"I guess you could say that."

Harry put his cackle on display again.

"Looks like you and me got a lot in common," the old man said.

"I guess I can't argue with that," Clint said.

"Does it surprise you?"

"Yeah it does," Clint said. "I always thought trouble just found me, but I'm starting to see that I get myself into trouble all by myself."

"Hey," Harry said, with a shrug, "we all gotta have somethin' to do."

"So suppose you tell me what's going on in this town."

"For another slab of ham, you got it."

# Chapter Eight

"Lemme start with Gentry, over at the Jack of Spades."

"He owns it and tends bar," Clint said.

"Right."

"What's he got up his sleeve?" Clint asked.

"There's a fella in town named Hiram Teach."

"What's his business?"

"What isn't?" Harry asked. "He owns a piece of the Jack of Spades, but also owns the Full House Saloon at the other end of town."

"So they're partners," Clint said.

"And they got plans to buy up more places," Harry said, "or just take 'em over."

"And you know this how?"

"They don't pay me no mind when I'm cleanin' up, so I hears everythin' they say."

"And what've they been saying?"

"They got a plan to make the Freight and Stage station a going concern by keeping the railroad out," Harry said. "But that ain't all."

"What else?"

"I ain't got it all yet," Harry said, "but they got plenty of plans."

"Are these just business takeovers," Clint asked, "or do you suspect something more violent?"

"Teach has his hired guns in his Full House all the time, ready and waitin' to be turned loose."

"And what's the sheriff think about this?"

"Now, he's the lawman, he's got every right to stick his nose in other people's business, but he don't. He just wantsta shoot stray dogs, make his rounds and collect his pay."

"So what else is going on?"

"I seen you with that pretty dress shop lady, Holly Clifford."

"She's got plans?" Clint asked, surprised.

"No," Harry said, "somebody's got plans for her."

"To take over her dress shop?" Clint laughed.

"Her father owns several businesses in town," Harry said. "He put the dress shop in her name, but he owns the Hardware Store, the Feed and Grain and—this'll interest you—the Gunsmith Shop."

"Tell me about two men named Larry and Caleb."

"You have a run in with them?" Harry asked.

"They were accosting the girl, Holly. I stepped in."

"Them fellas is two of Teach's guns."

"They didn't look eager to clear leather."

"They got orders to keep their guns in their holsters unless Teach says different," Harry said. "Of course, they didn't know who you was, or things mighta been different."

"Is that all?" Clint asked.

"Not hardly," Harry said. "I clean lots of places, including the mayor's office."

"And what's he got on his mind?"

"Holly's father, Benjamin, wants to run for Mayor next election," Harry said.

"What kind of chance would he have?"

"A good one," Harry said. "He's popular in town."

"What's the mayor think of that?"

"Our mayor is Big Bill Benedict," Harry said. "He's been mayor for twenty years and he ain't lookin' to step down any time soon."

"And what do Gentry and Teach have to do with the mayor?" Clint asked.

"You catch on quick," Harry said. "The mayor wouldn't mind if Teach turned his guns loose on Ben Clifford."

"He wants to stay in office that bad?" Clint asked. "Murder?"

"Whenever Teach's men draw their guns, there's witnesses who say it was self-defense."

"And they also work for Teach?"

"Yep."

"Is there a judge in town?"

"Judge Dodd," Harry said.

"And you clean his place, too?"

"No," Harry said, "he's got a woman who does that."

"And what does he think of all these things going on in town?"

"He's been a judge in town as long as Big Bill's been mayor."

"Are they a pair?"

"They put up with each other."

"This is a small town," Clint said. "Why are all these shenanigans going on?"

"There's talk of the railroad coming through here," Harry said. "That'll change the size of this place."

"It sure would."

"But it ain't a sure thing," Harry said. "Teach owns the Freight and Stage, so he don't want the railroad. That would kill his business."

"So what's he planning?"

"I don't know for sure, yet," Harry said. "Him and Gentry are plannin' somethin', though."

"Sounds like lots of people have lots of plans."

"And whatta you plan to do about it?" Harry asked.

"Why don't you tell me, Harry?"

# Chapter Nine

So Clint had made up his mind to get involved. He liked Harry Hayes, had a soft spot for Holly Clifford, already. It seemed as if her father, Ben Clifford, might be the only decent man in town.

"If I was you," Harry said, "I'd talk to Ben Clifford. He might have some ideas."

"I think you're right," Clint said. "But I might approach him through his daughter."

"You sweet on Holly already?"

"I just thought it would be easier."

"Yeah, well," Harry said, "you go ahead and play it your way."

"What are you going to do?" Clint asked.

"What I always do," Harry said. "Keep my ears open." He got to his feet. "Thanks for the breakfast."

Clint also stood, and the two men walked out the front door.

"You headin' for the Dress Shop?" Harry asked.

"Don't tell me you clean that place, too," Clint said.

"Naw, the little lady cleans her own place. Good luck. Let me know how it goes with Miss Clifford.

Harry went off in the opposite direction to swamp out his livery stable job.

Clint walked to Holly Clifford's dress shop. He took a moment to look at the dresses in the window, and then past them to Holly herself. He opened the door and stepped in as a bell tinkled above his head. Holly turned and smiled, lowering the dress she was holding.

"Mr. McCord."

"John, remember?"

"Of course. John, how nice to see you. Are you here to buy a dress for your wife?"

"I have no wife," he said, and then added, "and no one to buy a dress for."

"Then what brings you here?"

"You."

She raised her eyebrows and set the dress down.

"Oh?" she said. "What's on your mind?"

"I'd like to meet your father."

"Well," she said, "that's not a very flattering answer."

"I'm sorry for that," he said. "I should have asked you to dinner first."

"Perhaps you should have," she said, "but never mind. Why do you want to see my father?"

"It's come to my attention that he may be having some trouble."

"That might be true," she said, "but how do you know that?"

"I've not only been watching," he said, "but listening. And that's the word I hear."

"Why do you think you can help?" she asked.

"I've heard he might be in danger of facing some guns," Clint said. "Does your father carry a gun?"

"Never."

"Then he might need someone who does."

She looked him up and down.

"I can see that you do," she said, "but can you use it?"

"I can use it."

"Can you prove it?" she asked. "My father's a hard man to convince, sometimes."

"I can prove it."

She seemed to think it over before speaking again.

"I think I'll need a little more to even convince him to see you. He's a busy man. And a hard one."

"Maybe you should just tell him my name."

"John McCord?" she asked. "You think he'd recognize it?"

"He'd probably recognize my real name."

"Ah," she said, amused, "now we're getting somewhere. So what's your real name?"

"Clint Adams."

She lost the amused look and took a step back.

"You mean . . ."

"Yes."

". . . you're a gunfighter."

"That's what they say."

"Is-is it true?"

"It's not how I think of myself."

"B-but . . . you've killed so many men."

"I've killed men when they were trying to kill me," Clint said, "and it's not as many as they say."

"But you want to offer my father your gun?"

"My help," Clint said. "It doesn't have to be with a gun."

"But what else can you do for him?"

"That all depends on what his trouble is," Clint answered.

"Why did you tell me your name was McCord?"

"That's how I registered in the hotel," Clint said. "I wanted to relax before the word got out."

"And will it?"

"Are you going to tell anyone?"

"No, not if you don't want me to."

"Just your father."

"Yes, all right," she said. "I'll tell my father. Where will you be?"

"Sitting in front of the hotel," he said, "waiting."

# Chapter Ten

Clint sat the rest of the day in his chair, past dinner time. But he couldn't ignore his stomach and, finally, he rose to go for a meal. At that moment, he saw Holly crossing the street toward him.

"I've decided to let you take me to dinner," she said, "but it has to be the steak house."

"No problem," Clint said. "I'll buy you the biggest steak they've got."

They started to walk together.

"Have you spoken to your father yet?"

"Not yet," she said. "I've been in my shop all day. Tonight, I'll talk to him. But right now, we eat."

The waiter, used to having Clint there, took him to the same table.

"The usual for me," Clint said, "and get the lady whatever she wants."

"Mr. McCord promised me the largest steak you have."

"Coming up, Miss."

"Have you been here before?" Clint asked.

"Never," she said. "My shop is not as successful as I'd like, so I'm careful with my money."

"I thought an important man like your father would have plenty of money."

"He does," Holly said, "but it's his money. I have my own, what there is of it."

"I understand a railroad is going to come through here," he said. "That should increase your business."

"Yes if it comes," she said. "There are still lots of I's to dot and T's to cross before that happens."

"Sounds like it'll take some time."

"I'm afraid so."

"I hope you can keep your business going in the meantime." Clint had not seen any customers enter Holly's store all the days he had been sitting there.

"It will, if I have anything to say about it."

The waiter brought their steaks, surrounded by potatoes, carrots and onions. Holly's slab of meat was half the size of Clint's.

"Let's eat," he said attacking his.

Holly proceeded to eat, but she took very small cuts of meat, put them in her mouth and chewed slowly. At that rate, it would take hours to finish. But by the time Clint had finished his meal, Holly put her utensils down.

"Please wrap this up," she told the waiter, "I want to take it home."

"Yes, Miss."

As the waiter left with the plate, Clint asked, "For your father?"

"Yes," she said. "If I don't make him eat, he'd waste away."

"Do you always bring him food from a restaurant?"

"No," she said. "Usually I cook for him, but I'm not very good. This will be a treat for him, and I'll tell him that you paid."

\*\*\*

When they left the steakhouse Clint once again walked Holly home, only this time she knew her companion was the Gunsmith.

He walked her to the base of the stairway leading up. There was a light in the windows.

"You live here with your father?" he asked.

"Yes," she said, "when my mother died ten years ago, he sold our house and we moved here. He couldn't stand to be in that house without her. Good night, Clint. I'll have my father's answer for you in the morning. He'll want to know what you want in return."

"Nothing."

"You'll have to convince him of that."

"I'll do my best."

He watched her go up the stairs and through the door, then turned and walked away.

***

As Holly entered and closed the door behind her, her father barked out, "You're late! I'm hungry."

"I went to dinner," she said, "and brought you some leftovers."

"Leftovers?" He scowled. "From where?"

"The steakhouse."

"What?" His face brightened. "Gimme."

She handed him the tray she was carrying. He rushed to the table to uncover it.

"My God! Look at that."

"Sit down," she said, "and I'll bring you a knife and a fork."

"And coffee."

"Of course." She set the knife and fork down on the table, and he grabbed them up. "And I have a message for you."

"Well," he said, "sit down and tell me while I eat."

# Chapter Eleven

"Clint Adams?" Ben Clifford asked. "Are you sure?"

"Yes." She didn't know why she was sure, but she was.

"And what kind of trouble does he think I have?" Clifford asked.

"He's not sure, but he thinks it might involve guns."

"Well," Clifford said, "if it involves Hiram Teach, he's probably right."

"Does it involve Teach?" Holly asked. "What kind of trouble are you in?"

"Well, you know Big Bill doesn't want me to be mayor."

"Yes, I know," she said, "but would he have Teach kill you?"

"Teach, or his men," Clifford said.

"Father," Holly asked, "do you want to be mayor that bad?"

"This town needs somebody new, Holly," Clifford said, "and I'm the only one steppin' up."

She reached out and put her hand on her father's arm.

"I don't like it," she said. "Will you take help from Clint Adams?"

"That depends," her father said. "What's he want in return?"

"He says nothing."

"Well, that can't be true," he said.

"Then you ask him to explain it," she said. "I'm going to get comfortable, and then I'll clean up. You just go and sit."

"At my desk, yes," he said. "I have some work to do."

"You work too hard," she said.

"It's the only way I'm gonna get Big Bill out of office," he told her.

"You know, father," she said, "we could leave Firecreek, move on."

"I have too much invested here," Clifford told her. "I have to stay, but you could go."

"Not without you."

"I mean," he went on, "if you were to marry."

"There's nobody in this town I would marry," she said, "so I guess that's not going to happen." She sighed. "So I guess we're both stuck."

"Once I'm mayor, I'll get the railroad to come through here," he told her. "Then things will change for the better."

"I hope you're right."

"Tell Mr. Adams I'll see him tomorrow afternoon," he said.

"He paid for dinner tonight," she told him.

"Good," Clifford said, "I'll get him to buy me lunch."

"That would be taking advantage of him."

Now Ben Clifford sighed.

"All right, then," he said, "tell him to meet me at the steak house and *I'll* buy *him* lunch."

She smiled and said, "That's more like it." She bent over and kissed her father's forehead. "Don't work too late."

"I won't."

They both left the table, she to her room to get more comfortable, and he to his desk to think of a way he could put the Gunsmith to good use.

\*\*\*

Harry Hayes' last job of the night was always the mayor's office. He entered, carrying a pail, mop, and broom, and was surprised to see the mayor still at his desk.

Big Bill Benedict had always been a big man, hence his name. But as he got older, he continued to fill out, so that these days folks in town had started calling him "Fat" Bill, behind his back.

"Oh, sorry, Mr. Mayor," Harry said. "I didn't think you'd be here."

"Just winding up a few things, Harry," Benedict said. "I'll be done in a few minutes. "While you wait, get yourself a drink."

"Don't mind if I do."

He went to the mayor's sideboard, where he had several bottles. Harry chose the brandy and poured himself a healthy swig.

While he drank, he heard several sighs from the mayor, and knew something was weighing heavily on him.

"Problems, Mr. Mayor?" he asked.

"That's all my days are filled with, Harry," Benedict said. "Problems."

"That's too bad."

The mayor folded his hands on the desk and looked at Harry.

"Sometimes I think you've got it made, Harry," he said.

"Me?"

"Your biggest problem is where to clean first," Benedict went on. "And nobody in town wants your job."

"I guess you're right," Harry said. He finished his brandy and set the glass down. "You want me to come back later?"

"No, no," Benedict said, getting to his feet with some difficulty, "I'm leaving. I've got to get out to the steak house for the final seating." He headed for the door. "Have a good night, Harry."

After the mayor had left, Harry poured himself another drink, walked to the man's desk, and started looking at the papers he had left behind.

# Chapter Twelve

In the morning, Clint went out to his chair after breakfast. He told Holly he'd be waiting for her there. Before long he saw Holly Clifford crossing the street toward him. He stood to greet her.

"Good morning," he said.

" 'morning, Clint."

"How did your father enjoy his dinner?"

"He was very pleased."

"And you told him about me?" Clint asked.

"I did."

"What did he say?"

"He'd like to buy you lunch today," she said. "At the steak house."

"That sounds good. What time?"

"Meet him there at one."

"And will you be there, as well?"

"No," Holly said, "my father does his business alone."

"But can I see you again, after?"

She looked down and said, "If you like." Now she looked at him. "I'll be in my shop til six."

"Then I'll see you there."

"Good," she said. "You can tell me how your lunch with my father went."

"I will."

"And I'll thank you now for your offer of help," she said. She kissed his cheek, then ran back across the street to her shop.

At the same time, Harry Hayes came out of the Jack of Spades Saloon, this time under his own power, with his coins in hand. He also came across the street to Clint.

"It looks like you're doin' well with Holly," he said.

"She's arranged a meeting for me with her father."

"He's a good man," Harry said. "He'll make a good mayor, if he manages to unseat Big Bill."

"What can you tell me about the mayor?"

"He's a tired man," Harry said. "He left me alone in his office last night, with papers on the desk."

"What were the papers for?"

"He's been in touch with the railroad," Harry said. "He's trying to convince them to turn their attention east or west of here. If they bypass Firecreek, he'll probably stay mayor. Or he'll arrange for someone else to take his place."

"Like Teach?"

"He's tired enough to do that," Harry said. "It would be the worst thing for this town."

"Well," Clint said, "let's see what Ben Clifford has to say at lunch."

"I'll be interested," Harry said.

"Have you had any conversations with Clifford?" Clint asked.

"Nobody talks to me, Mr. Adams," Harry said. "I'm just the old swamper."

"And you prefer it that way, don't you?"

"I do," Harry said. "Nothin's expected from me, and I like it that way, too."

"Then why talk to me?"

"Why not?" Harry replied. "You can get things done."

"And you can't?"

"Like I said, nobody takes me serious," Harry said.

"I do," Clint replied.

"That's because you're a stranger here," Harry said, "and you've been watchin'. But you're finished with watchin', aint'cha?"

Clint sighed and said, "I'm afraid so."

"Why afraid?"

"I thought I was done sticking my nose into other people's business," Clint said. "Now I discover it's a hard habit to break."

"You see?" Harry said. "It's a hard habit for me to break bein' a nobody who no one pays attention to." He didn't tell Clint about his short exchange with the mayor.

"Harry," Clint said, "I get the feeling you could run this town."

"I don't wanna do that," Harry said. "I just wanna live here. Don't you go gettin' no ideas about tellin' people about me."

"I wouldn't do that," Clint said. "That'd be up to you. And likewise, don't be telling anyone about me."

"You got a deal." Harry picked up his bucket. "I got a stable to clean. You have a good lunch."

The old man walked away to his livery stable job. Clint decided to sit right back down until lunchtime.

What else was there to do?

\*\*\*

At quarter-to-one Clint stood up and started walking to the steak house. He was very interested in this meeting with Holly's father, Ben Clifford. This meeting might be the beginning of his change from watching to doing.

# Chapter Thirteen

"Mr. McCord," the waiter greeted him at the door. "Lunch?"

"I'm meeting Ben Clifford here," Clint said.

"Ah, yes, this way," the waiter said, and led him across a crowded room. Apparently, the steak house was just as popular for lunch as it was for dinner.

The waiter led Clint to a table occupied by a rough-hewn man in his late fifties, with close cut, salt-and-pepper hair and a granite jaw.

"Mr. Clifford?" the waiter said. "Mr. McCord."

"Ah, yes," the man said, rising, "Mr. McCord." He extended his hand, and they shook. "Please, sit. I haven't ordered yet."

Clint sat across from the man.

"Steak?" Clifford asked.

"What else?" Clint replied.

Clifford looked at the waiter and said, "Two steaks."

"Yes, Sir. Both bloody?"

Clifford looked at Clint, who nodded.

"Yes," Clifford said, "bloody. And two mugs of beer."

"Yes, Sir. Right away."

As the waiter walked away, Cliford looked at Clint and asked, "Are we sticking with McCord?"

"For now," Clint said. "We don't need the extra attention."

"We're pretty private here," Clifford said. "I like to keep my table away from others."

"Same here."

"So," Clifford said, "Holly says you want to help me. Just what is it you think I need help with?"

"I've been here a few days and I've heard some things," Clint said.

"From Harry Hayes?"

"How do you know that?"

Clifford smiled.

"I've known Harry a long time," he said. "Nobody knows what's going on in this town like Harry does."

"I don't believe he thinks anyone knows that," Clint commented.

"Harry's very closemouthed, but I know he sees and hears everything." Clifford said.

"Well, he tells me you're looking to get the mayor out of office and put yourself in there."

"My first goal is to get him out," the man said. "I don't necessarily want to replace him, but if no one else steps up, I may have no choice."

"And how do you think the mayor is going to respond to your threat to replace him?"

"Have you heard anything about a man named Teach?" Clifford asked.

"I have," Clint said. "I've heard about him and Race Gentry."

"Race is happy to own his saloon, but Teach wants more," Clifford said. "He's been Big Bill's man for some time, but he's looking to move on from Bill."

"Then does he want him in office or out?"

"I'd like to ask Harry about that," Clifford said. "Whatever his main goal is, he's got his own gunmen and isn't afraid to use them."

"Do you think he'd send them after you?"

"It wouldn't surprise me," Clifford said.

"Are you afraid of being bushwhacked?"

"No," Clifford said, "they'd make it look like a fair fight."

"But you don't wear a gun."

"Teach has done away with a couple of thorns in his side, even though they didn't wear guns."

"Fair fights?"

"Every time."

"What'd the sheriff say?"

"What does he always say?" Clifford replied. "That's somebody else I want to see replaced. Hey, would you be interested?"

"Not in wearing a badge," Clint said. "I've already got a target on my back."

"Must be a tough way to live," Clifford said.

"Well, it seems like you're walking around wearing one, too."

"These days, I feel that way," Clifford said. "But they'll come at me head on, when they come."

"Have you talked to Teach about it?"

"I haven't exchanged a word with Hiram Teach in a month of Sundays."

"You don't go to his saloon?"

"Never."

"Where do you do your drinking?"

"At home," Clifford said. "I won't give Race Gentry my business, either."

"Mr. Clifford," Clint said, as the waiter returned with their plates, "who's on your side?"

"Nobody I can think of."

"Then how do you expect to beat Big Bill for mayor?" Clint asked.

"Folks don't have to stand with me," Clifford said. "When they vote, they vote in private, so nobody'll know."

"When's the next election?"

"A few months."

The waiter brought their beers, and they started eating, each alone with his thoughts for a while.

# Chapter Fourteen

"What is it you think you can do for me . . . McCord?" Clifford asked over coffee.

"It occurs to me somebody should talk to Mr. Teach," Clint answered.

"Are you going to threaten him with your gun?"

"I don't use my gun unless somebody skins one on me."

"Teach wouldn't do that," Clifford said. "He'd send some of his boys."

"I met a couple of yahoos named Larry and Caleb," Clint said. "Are they his?"

"Is that the Larry that's after my Holly?" the man asked.

"I believe so," Clint said. "I had to chase them off, one day."

"Well, I believe Larry's one of Teach's boys," Clifford said. "I don't know anybody named Caleb."

"What about Big Bill?" Clint asked. "You talk to him?"

"We exchange pleasantries," Clifford said. "He wouldn't come right out and threaten me. He'd leave that to Teach."

"Well," Clint said, if it's all right with you, I'll go and meet Hiram Teach."

"As McCord, or as Clint Adams?"

"I think I'd do the most good as Clint Adams."

"He's going to think I hired you for your gun," Clifford pointed out.

"I'll change his mind."

Clint started to get up, but Clifford said, "I've got one more question."

Clint sat and asked, "What's that?"

"Why get involved?" the man asked. "You're just passing through. Why not just keep passing?"

"That's a good question," Clint said. "I'm having some trouble answering that, myself."

"Are you just bored?"

"That might be part of it," Clint said. "I thought I might enjoy just sitting and watching, but that got old fast, and then I started talking to Harry."

"Good old Harry," Clifford said. "He started telling you stories, ay?"

"Is that what they are," Clint said, "just stories?"

"Well, if he told you about me, and Big Bill, and Teach, I guess there's some truth in what Harry says. Of course, that depends on what else he's told you."

"Why don't we just start with this," Clint suggested.

"And what do you want in return?" Clifford asked.

"I guess I was just looking for something to do."

"So, no fee for your services?"

"No fee," Clint agreed.

They stood up and left the steak house together.

"Are you going to talk to Teach now?" Clifford asked.

"No time like the present."

"You going alone?"

"You know anybody in town who might back me up?" Clint asked.

"To tell you the truth, no," Clifford said, "especially not me. I'm no hand with a gun."

"What about a rifle?"

"I can hunt, but that's about it."

Clint shrugged.

"Then I guess I'm going alone."

"Just keep a sharp eye on Teach," Clifford said. "He's got a few different little moves he uses to set his men off."

"I'll keep an eye on him."

"I'm going back home to do some paperwork. You go to the Full. There can't be much business."

"That'll make it easier to watch Teach and his men," Clint said.

"Let me know what happens."

They stepped off the boardwalk and each went their own way.

\*\*\*

The Full House looked well cared for on the outside. The name of the place was painted in bright red over the doorway. He went through the batwing doors and saw that Clifford was right. There were only a few customers at the bar and none at the tables. One table had two men sitting at it, but they weren't customers. He recognized them as Larry and Caleb.

He walked to the bar, where a tired looking bartender came over. He could've been forty or sixty, he was so worn out.

"Getcha somethin'?" he asked.

"A beer," Clint said, "and the boss."

"I kin give ya the beer right here," the bartender said. He drew it and set it in front of Clint. "The boss is upstairs."

Clint sipped the cold beer and said, "Can you send one of those boys upstairs to get him?"

"What fer?"

"I want to see him."

"And who're you?"

Clint sipped the beer again and said, "My name's Clint Adams."

The bartender stared at him, and then said, "It ain't not."

# Chapter Fifteen

The bartender came out from behind the bar and walked over to the table where Larry and Caleb were sitting. He must have told them Clint's name, because they both sat up straighter and looked across the floor at him. Clint leaned on the bar and raised his glass to them.

The bartender came back to the bar, and the two men stood up and walked over, got on either side of Clint.

"Now that you know who I am," Clint said. "I'm going to ask you both to stand to one side of me."

They hesitated, then Caleb moved over and stood next to Larry.

"You expect us to believe you're the Gunsmith?" Larry asked.

"I'm not asking you to believe it. I just want to talk to your boss. So one of you hurry upstairs and tell him I'm here, and we'll see what he believes."

The two men stared at him, and then Larry said, "Caleb, go on up and tell Mr. Teach the Gunsmith is here. Let's see what he says."

Caleb went up the stairs.

***

Hiram Teach pulled on his boots, turned and looked over his shoulder at the naked woman in his bed. She was lying with her back to him, which was good, because she looked better that way. Her forty years were starting to show on her face, but her body was still good. He followed the line of her back down to the cleft between her chunky buttocks. She was what most men would call "a fine-lookin' woman."  But her days were numbered.

"Come on, Alma," he said. "Time to get up and start your day."

She rolled onto her back, her big breasts falling to opposite sides. She opened one eye, then the other and stared at him. Mornings were not kind to her.

"Hiram," she said, "when are you gonna marry me so I don't have to wait tables no more?"

"Now, you know I'm not the marrying kind, Alma," he said. He slapped her on one meaty thigh and stood up. "Now get dressed."

She slipped one of her hands down between her legs and said, "You sure. I'm kinda wet."

She held her hand out to him and he saw her juices glistening on her fingertips.

"Get dried off, woman," he said. "Save it for tonight."

There was a knock at his door at that point. Alma reached down and pulled the sheet over her.

Treat walked to the door and opened it.

"What do you want, Caleb?" he demanded.

Caleb sneaked a look past him, at Alma, then said, "Fella downstairs wants to see ya, boss."

"What fella," Treat asked, "and what's he want to see me about?"

"He didn't say what it was about," Caleb said, "but he says he's Clint Adams."

Treat frowned.

"The Gunsmith?"

"That's who he claims to be."

Treat thought a moment, then said, "Tell 'im I'll be right down."

"Yessir."

Caleb took one more look at Alma before Treat closed the door.

"The Gunsmith's here to see you?" Alma asked. "You better set your boys on him, Hiram."

"If he's the Gunsmith," Teach said, "I just might do that."

He slipped into his jacket and left the room.

***

Clint watched the stairs, saw Caleb come down first.

"He'll be along," Caleb said, coming to the bar.

"I better get his breakfast ready," the bartender said.

"Breakfast?" Clint asked. "It's after lunch time."

"Not for the boss," the bartender said. He went through a doorway behind the bar that, presumably, led to a kitchen.

Clint finished his beer while keeping one eye on the stairs, and the other on the two gunmen. Eventually, a man appeared on the stairs and came down.

"Mr. Adams?" he asked, as he approached Clint.

"That's right."

"Let me get this straight," Teach said. "You're the Gunsmith?"

"That's right."

"Why should I believe you?"

"Who would lie about that," Clint asked, "and paint a target on their back?"

"I suppose that's true enough."

The man was tall, in his forties, looked to be in fine shape. He extended his hand and Clint shook, finding the handshake firm.

"Join me at my table, Mr. Adams," he said.

"Thank you."

Teach looked at his men and said, "You boys get on about your day."

"You sure, boss?" Larry asked.

"I'm sure Mr. Adams is not here to shoot me," Teach said. "Now go on."

As Teach led Clint to a back table, Larry and Caleb left the saloon.

# Chapter Sixteen

As the bartender brought out a plate of eggs for Teach, the man said, "I hope you don't mind if I eat breakfast while we talk. I keep late hours."

"No problem," Clint said.

"Would you like some coffee?" Teach asked.

"That'd be fine."

"Andy, bring Mr. Adams some coffee."

"Yes, Sir."

"Now," Teach said, attacking his eggs, "suppose you tell me why you're here?"

"I've had a conversation with Ben Clifford," Clint said.

"Ah," Teach said, "what horrible things has Clifford told you about me?"

"Just that you'd do just about anything to keep him from unseating the present mayor."

"Big Bill has been mayor for a very long time," Teach said. "He's kept this town alive."

"It seems there's a question about the railroad coming in," Clint said. "The mayor doesn't want it. Why would that be?"

"Big Bill feels we can get along just fine without the railroad," Teach said.

"And what about you?" Clint asked. "The railroad wouldn't do your Freight and Stage company much good."

"No, it wouldn't, at that," Teach said, "but I'd start a business to replace it. There's always something."

"So, you'll support the present mayor in the next election," Clint said.

"And in every election after that, as long as he runs."

"And Clifford?"

"If he runs, he won't win."

"You'll see to that?"

"If you're asking me if I'd have him killed to keep him out of office, that's preposterous."

"You do have gunmen in your employ, like those two who just left?"

"Larry and Caleb?" Teach laughed. "They're boys, Mr. Adams, not gunmen."

"But you do have men."

"I have employees," Teach said. "They're involved in several of my businesses."

Clint drank his coffee.

"Are you here to tell me you're working for Ben Clifford? You're *his* gun?"

"I don't sell my gun, Mr. Teach," Clint said. "I'm just getting the lay of the land."

"You haven't gotten enough from Harry Hayes?" Teach asked.

"The old swamper?"

Teach laughed.

"That's how Harry wants everyone in town to think of him," Teach said. "But old Harry's got his thumb in a lot of pies."

"I had a talk with Clifford," Clint said, "not Harry Hayes."

"Come on," Teach said. "Someone put you on to Clifford. You telling me it wasn't ol' Harry?"

"I'm not telling you anything," Clint said. "I'm just asking."

Teach put his fork down and sat back in his chair.

"I think I get it, now," he said.

"Get what?"

"It's Holly," Teach said. "You and Clifford's daughter are . . . involved? And she set you up with her father."

"Holly's a nice girl," Clint said, "but I'm not, as you say, 'involved' with her."

"Whatever you say," Teach said. "I think we're finished here. If you wanted to tell me you're backing Ben Clifford, you did that. I don't know how much he's paying you—"

69

"Stop right there," Clint said. "I'm not being paid. I'm just satisfying my own curiosity."

"Oh, I see," Teach said. "Well, thank you for coming by, but I have to get to work."

"In your many businesses?"

"I'm a businessman, yes," Teach said, "which means I'm very busy." He stood up. "Have a good day, Mr. Adams."

Teach turned and walked to a door in the back wall, and through it. Clint assumed that was his office.

He stood and walked to the bar.

"We're gettin' ready to do some heavy business, Mister," Andy, the bartender, said. "You want somethin'?"

At that moment a woman wearing a plain, yellow cotton dress, came down the stairs and walked past the bar.

" 'mornin', Andy," she said, giving Clint a long look before going out the door. Clint thought she had been quite beautiful once but had lived a hard life. Still, she was a fine-looking woman.

"That's Alma," Andy said, "the boss's woman, so don't get any ideas."

"No ideas here, Andy," Clint said. "None at all."

"If you ain't gonna order somethin', you hafta go," Andy said. "We're gonna get busy."

Clint looked around and said, "I can see that, Andy. I can see it."

He left the Full House Saloon.

# Chapter Seventeen

From the Full House Clint went directly to Holly Clifford's dress shop. He walked in, the bell tinkling above his head. Holly was dealing with a middle-aged woman who was buying some cloth. Clint waited until they were finished, and held the door open for the woman. Holly then walked to the door and turned her OPEN sign to CLOSED.

"That was a long lunch."

"Lunch with your father, and breakfast with Hiram Teach."

"Teach!" Holly spat. "He's a horrible man."

"I didn't see that side of him," Clint said, "but I can believe it."

She walked around behind her counter and leaned on it.

"How'd you get along with my father?"

"Okay, I guess," Clint said. "I think I convinced him I didn't want anything from him."

"Just to be helpful, huh?"

"Sounds like I've got to convince you, too."

"No, no," she said waving a hand, "I believe you. What did you agree to do for him?"

"Just talk to Teach," Clint said, "let him know I was here."

"You told Teach your real name?"

"I did."

"How did he take it?"

"He took it pretty well."

"Did he have his men around him?" she asked.

"Nope," Clint said. "Just him and his bartender."

"And a shotgun under the bar."

"I'm sure there was, but there was no need," Clint said, "We just talked."

"About what?"

"Your father, the mayor, a little bit about Harry Hayes."

"What about Harry?" she asked.

"More people know more about him than he thinks," Clint said. "Or maybe he is aware."

"He's a sharp old man," she said. "People think he's addled because of what he does."

"And it's because of what he does that he hears a lot," Clint said.

"What can he do with what he hears?" she asked.

"I don't think he's made up his mind about that, yet," Clint said.

"Well," she said, "what do you plan to do now?"

"I satisfied my curiosity," he said. "At least, some of it. But I won't be here when the next election rolls around."

"Well then, do me a favor while you are here," she said.

"What's that?"

"Convince my father to forget about running for mayor," she told him. "Just get him to continue doing business and forget about politics."

"I don't think I can do that," Clint said.

"Why?"

"Your father seems to have a mind of his own."

"That's for sure," she said. "Then maybe you can figure out a way around his pigheadedness."

"I guess I can try."

"Now," she said, coming around the counter to stand in front of him, "about you and me."

"I told Teach there was nothing between us," Clint told her.

"It wasn't a lie," she said. "There is nothing between us . . . or there wasn't, until now."

She put her arms around his neck and pulled him down into a deep, searching kiss that went on for some time.

When she broke the kiss she said, "You know I live with my father."

"I do."

"Then do you have a suggestion that doesn't involve the floor of my back room?"

He smiled and said, "I do."

\*\*\*

Clint took Holly to his hotel, and up to his room, where they went back to kissing before they started removing each other's clothes.

Holly was a tall, well-built young woman with pale, satiny skin. He waited until he had her totally naked before removing his gunbelt and hanging it on the bedpost. She watched from the bed while he took a wooden chair and shoved the back of it beneath the doorknob, then removed his boots and clothes.

"This is how you always live, isn't it?" she asked. "So careful?"

He got into bed with her.

"I like living," he said. "Careful is life."

"Do you think I'm in danger?" she asked. "Is someone going to try to break in?"

"I'd do this even if you weren't here," he said.

"You mean . . . this?" She grabbed his hard cock.

"No," he said, "not this." He bit her breasts, first one, then the other.

She laughed and he rolled on top of her.

# Chapter Eighteen

Once they began to make love, Clint discovered Holly Clifford was not the prim and proper dressmaker she pretended to be. . . at least, not in bed.

She rolled him onto his back and then worked her way down his body with kisses. He was surprised that she knew exactly what she was doing. But he stopped wondering about it and just settled back to enjoy it.

She got down between his legs and began to lick his hard cock. She caressed him with her hands while licking, then took him into her mouth and began sucking. He took as much of that as he could, then reached down and pulled her up on top of him. With a twitch of her hips she took him inside her wet pussy and started to ride him, grunting every time she came down on him.

He took her hips in his hands and started to match her movements. Suddenly she shuddered, her body went taut and, just before he exploded into her, she collapsed on him . . .

They remained that way for a while, and then she slid off of him.

"I have to go," she said, breathlessly.

"Wait," he said, reaching for her. "There's things I want to do . . ."

She laughed and moved away from him.

"I have to go."

"Why?"

"My shop," she said, "I have to reopen my shop."

She stood up, grabbed a nearby towel to wipe between her legs, and then got dressed.

"Holly . . ." he said, getting to his feet.

She smiled at him and pressed her hands to his naked chest.

"I knew this was going to happen," she said. "Next time we'll spend more time together."

"Next time?"

"Oh, yes," she said, "there's definitely going to be a next time.

"What about your father?"

"No, he can't know about this," she said. "You help him all you can, but it's got nothing to do with you and me. That's different. Understand? This is between you and me."

"I understand."

She kissed him again, then turned and left. He could hear her hurried footsteps out in the hall.

\*\*\*

Harry Hayes saw Clint and Holly go into the hotel. It wasn't hard to figure what they were going to do. If Ben Clifford found out about it, there would be trouble for sure. He wasn't going to tell him, but somebody might. When he got a chance, he would warn Clint Adams. Ben Clifford was a quiet man, and a calm man, except when it came to his daughter.

He would warn Clint as soon as he could.

\*\*\*

Hiram Teach sat at his table in The Full House Saloon. When Larry and Caleb came back in, he waved them over.

"Sit down, boys," he said. "I've got some things to tell you. Larry, go get us some beers."

"Yessir."

Larry went to the bar, while Caleb sat across from his boss.

"What's up, boss?" he asked.

"We've got two problems," Teach said. "One is Clint Adams."

"What?" That was the first time Caleb had heard Clint's real name. "The Gunsmith's in town?"

"That was him I've been talking to," Teach said.

"What's goin' on?" Larry asked, putting the beers on the table and sitting.

"That feller who chased us away from Holly," Caleb said. "He's Clint Adams."

Larry's eyes went wide.

"Hey," he said, "we coulda killed us the Gunsmith."

"Don't fool yourselves," Teach said. "He would've killed you both, easy."

"Mebbe not," Larry said. "I'm pretty fast."

"We don't need somebody pretty fast," Teach said, "we need someone fast as lightning."

"And who would that be?" Caleb asked.

"I'm working on that," Teach said, "but I want you boys to take care of the other problem."

"What's that?" Caleb asked.

"Harry Hayes."

"The old saloon swamper?" Caleb said. "Why's he a problem?"

"Because he knows everything that goes on in this town," Teach said.

"He's lived here a long time," Larry said.

"I know," Teach said, "and we've let him have his way too long."

"But if he's been here so long, why's he a problem now?" Caleb asked.

"Because he's starting to talk," Teach said.

"So whatta you wanna do?" Larry asked.

Teach drank some beer and said, "I want him to stop talking."

# Chapter Nineteen

Harry Hayes had just finished one of his jobs and was moving to the next one. He was cutting through an alley when a man appeared in front of him. When he turned to go back the other way, a second man appeared. He was boxed in and all he had was a mop and broom, in a bucket.

"Whatta you fellas want?" he asked.

They closed in on him, until he was backed up against a wall.

"We hear you know a lot about what goes on in town," Larry said.

"Me?" Harry asked. "I'm just a swamper."

"Yeah, you clean," Caleb said, "but you also listen."

"And lately," Larry said, "you talk too much."

"I don't talk to nobody," Harry insisted.

"You been talkin' to the Gunsmith," Caleb said. "That's not a good thing."

"Whatayou want from me?" Harry asked.

"Simple," Larry said. "We're here to make sure you stop talkin'."

"I ain't gonna talk," Harry said. "I swear."

"We're gonna make sure," Caleb said.

They both started punching Harry Hayes, in the face, the chest, the stomach, until he slumped to the dirt floor of the alley, his face a bloody mess.

"That's enough!" Caleb snapped. While he stopped, Larry started kicking the prone Harry Hayes. "Larry! Enough!"

Caleb pulled Larry away from Hayes, then bent to examine the old man.

"Aw, Christ!" he said.

"Whatsa matter?" Larry asked.

"He's dead."

"So what?" Larry asked. "The boss didn't want him talkin' to anybody. Now he won't."

"I-I guess you're right," Caleb said, looking around. "Come on, we better get outta here."

Larry headed for the front of the alley.

"No," Caleb said, "that way." He pointed to the back. "We don't wanna be seen."

Both men looked down at the dead man one more time, then ran toward the back of the alley.

\*\*\*

"He's what?" Teach asked.

"Um," Caleb said, "he's dead."

"Did I tell you to kill him?" Teach asked.

They were in Hiram Teach's office, his two men standing in front of his desk, their heads bowed.

"No, Sir," Caleb said, "but . . . we only meant to make our point."

"So you beat him to death?" Teach demanded.

"Um," Larry said, "we beat him, and he died."

"How is that different from what I just said?" Teach demanded.

"Well," Caleb said, "we didn't mean to kill him."

"You!" Teach snapped, pointing at Larry. "Out!"

"Y-yessir."

Larry left the office.

"Caleb, what the hell happened?"

"Larry got carried away, Sir," Caleb said. "I tried to stop him, but he kept hitting the old man, and when he fell to the ground, he started kickin' him."

"And you just watched?"

"By the time I pulled him off, the old man was dead," Caleb said. "I'm sorry, Sir, but . . . but he ain't gonna talk."

"No, he's not," Teach said. "And neither is Larry. Do you get my meaning? Or do I have to make it plainer?"

"No, Sir," Caleb said. "I get it. You want me to take care of Larry."

"Yes," Teach said, "and right away."

"Yessir."

Caleb turned and left the office.

\*\*\*

When Larry left the office, he went to the bar for a drink.

"You got blood on ya," the bartender said.

"Yeah, I know," Larry said. "I gotta get cleaned up."

Caleb came out of the office then and joined Larry at the bar. He heard what he said.

"We both gotta get cleaned up," he agreed.

"You ain't got so much on you," Larry pointed out.

"Let's go in the back room." He looked at the bartender. "Bring us a bucket of water and some towels."

They walked across the room, attracting curious stares from the room full of customers.

Larry and Caleb entered the back storeroom, with Caleb bringing up the rear. He was able to take out his knife and jam it into Larry's back. The younger man stiffened, and then slumped to the floor.

"You ain't gonna talk either, friend," Caleb said.

He waited for the bartender to join him and help dispose of the body.

# Chapter Twenty

Clint was still in his room when there was a knock on his door. He was fully dressed except for his gun. He grabbed it from the bedpost, strapped it on and went to the door.

"Who is it?"

"Sheriff Harlow."

Clint opened the door, and saw the sheriff standing there alone.

"What can I do for you, Sheriff?" Clint asked.

"You can come with me, Mr. McCord," the lawman said. "I've got somethin' I wanna show you."

"Okay," Clint said, stepping into the hall, "lead the way."

He followed the man out of the hotel and down the street to the mouth of an alley, where a bunch of people were assembled.

"What's going on?" he asked.

"You'll see."

Harlow led him past the people, into the alley, where a man's body was lying. Clint could immediately see it was Harry Hayes.

"Aw no," he said.

"When's the last time you saw Harry?" Harlow asked.

"This morning."

"Did he say anythin' to you about bein' in trouble?"

"Not a word."

"And I suppose you know nothin' about this," Harlow said.

"As much as you do," Clint said. Harlow was still calling him McCord, so no one had told him Clint's real name. "Who do you think did it?"

"Well," Harlow said, "since it's Harry, we know it wasn't a robbery."

"So somebody killed him for no reason?" Clint asked.

"There had to be a reason," Harlow said. "If I can find that out, maybe I can find out who did it."

"You mean, you're going to look for the killer?"

"I liked Harry," Harlow said, "so yeah, I am."

"I liked Harry, too," Clint said, "so let me know if there's anything I can do."

"I'll take you up on that, Mr. McCord."

"The name's Adams," Clint said, "Clint Adams."

Harlow looked surprised, but not shocked.

"I had a feeling you were usin' a phony name, but I'm surprised the Gunsmith is in Firecreek. Any particular reason?"

"Not when I got here," Clint said, "but this sort of changes things."

"I'll accept any help you wanna give me," Harlow said.

"If I was you, I'd talk to Hiram Teach."

Harlow rubbed his jaw.

"That's somethin' I try my best never to do."

"Then I'll go with you, if you like."

"Yeah," Harlow said, "yeah, I'll take you up on that. Lemme get Harry moved to the undertaker, and then we'll go to the Full House."

"You got it."

Harlow collected some men from the rabble standing at the mouth of the alley and had them pick up the body and carry it to the undertaker.

"Okay," he said to Clint, "let's go."

\*\*\*

When they reached the Full House Saloon, there was a lot of activity inside. Clint and Harlow walked to the bar.

"Sheriff," the man said. "We don't usually see you in here."

"I wanna see Mr. Teach," Harlow said. "Where is he?"

"In his office," the bartender said, inclining his head, "back there. Knock before you go in."

Clint and Harlow made their way to the door and the lawman knocked.

"Come in!"

They opened the door and entered.

"Gentlemen," Teach greeted, from behind his desk. "What can I do for you?"

"Harry Hayes is dead," Harlow said.

"That's a shame. What happened?"

"Somebody beat him to death," the lawman said.

"And why are you here?"

"Mr. Adams suggested I talk to you about it."

"Is that right? I see Mr. Adams has properly introduced himself to you." Teach looked at Adams. "Why point the sheriff in my direction, Adams?"

"Because you have the men who would do something like this," Clint said. "All you'd have to do is point them."

"If I find out that any of my men did this, I'll hand them over to you, Sheriff," Teach said. "It's not my style to beat a helpless old man to death."

"What if that old man knew some things about you, Teach?" Clint asked.

Teach shrugged.

"What is there to know?" he asked. "I'm a business-man."

Harlow looked at Clint.

"What about your two men?" Clint asked.

"I have more than two men working for me," Teach said.

"I'm talking about Larry and Caleb."

"Larry Morris and Caleb Tarr, you mean," Teach said. "I don't know where they are, at the moment. If you want to question them, you'll have to find them."

"I think we'll do that," Clint said.

"Sheriff," Teach said, "have you deputized Adams?"

"I don't need a badge to do what I can to help," Clint said.

"I guess not," Teach said. "Is there anything else I can do for you?"

Harlow looked at Clint again and shook his head.

"Not right now," the lawman said. "Thanks for your time."

"My pleasure, gents."

Harlow and Clint left the office, crossed the crowded floor to the batwing doors and left.

Outside they stopped and Harlow asked, "Whattaya think?"

"Harry thought Teach was involved in something, but he said he hadn't heard everything."

"What *did* he hear?"

"He didn't tell me exactly, but I think it has something to do with Ben Clifford, and the next mayoral election."

Harlow made a face and said, "I was afraid you were gonna say somethin' like that."

# Chapter Twenty-One

Harlow and Clint's next stop was Ben Clifford's hardware store. As they entered, Clifford was finishing with a customer.

"Gents," Clifford said, as the customer turned to leave, "it's a little odd to see you two together."

"Mr. Adams has agreed to help me with a little problem I have," Harlow said.

"And that is?"

"Harry Hayes was beaten to death in an alley," Clint said.

"Oh, Jesus," Clifford said. "Poor old sod. Any idea who did it?"

"Do *you* have any idea?" Harlow asked.

"Well, if I was you, I'd talk to Hiram Teach," Clifford said. "He's got some men who like beating people up, not to mention killing them."

"We just came from there," Clint said.

"Now we're here," Harlow said.

"I don't know what you want from me," Clifford said. "I'd have no reason to kill Harry Hayes. I liked the old guy."

Harlow looked at Clint, who shrugged.

"Then we'll leave you alone, Mr. Clifford," Harlow said, "and look elsewhere."

"I know you said you spoke with Teach already, but I'd look very closely at him."

"We intend to," Harlow said. "Thanks for seein' us."

"Anything I can do, just let me know," Clifford said.

"We will."

Harlow and Clint left the hardware store and stopped just outside.

"Now what?" Harlow asked. "I don't know who else to talk to."

"We have to find those two men on Teach's payroll, Larry and Caleb."

"Okay," Harlow said, "where do we look?"

"Are there any other saloons in town besides the Jack of Spades, and the Full House?" Clint asked.

"A couple of smaller ones," Harlow said.

"Good," Clint said, "let's start there. Lead the way."

***

The first saloon was down a side street, where nobody would be able to find it by accident. It was called The Palace.

"Is this a joke?" Clint asked, looking at the rundown exterior.

"Probably not at the time they opened," Harlow said, "but it is, now."

They entered and Clint saw that inside was even more of a mess than the outside. Several of the tables were standing on three legs, and the bar was slanted so that glasses would slide off if they weren't held.

"You know what these boys look like, right?" Harlow asked.

"You don't?"

"I might recognize them on sight, but not by name."

"I know them," Clint assured him.

They walked to the bar.

"Drinks?" the bartender asked, as they approached.

"Not a chance," Clint said. "We're looking for two men, named Larry and Caleb."

"I know 'em," the bartender said, "but I ain't seen 'em lately."

Clint looked around the room, at the few customers who were there.

"Okay," he said to Harlow, "let's go."

Outside Clint asked, "What's next?"

"A place called the Silver Blade."

"Lead the way," Clint said.

# Chapter Twenty-Two

The Silver Blade was as rundown as the Palace and had even fewer customers.

"What's the law doin' here?" the bartender demanded.

"Never mind," Clint said, "we're looking for two men named Larry and Caleb."

The bartender looked at them suspiciously.

"What for?" he asked.

"Never mind," Harlow said. "Have you seen them?"

"You better talk to the boss. Wait here."

The bartender came around from behind the bar and hurried to the back of the saloon. When he returned, he had an older man following him.

"You better come with me, Sheriff," the older man said.

"What's goin' on, Elliot?"

"You'll see."

Dan Elliot led Clint and Harlow to a back room, and to the back door of the Blade.

"We just found him about an hour ago. We were still wonderin' what to do."

He opened the back door and allowed Clint and Harlow to go through. They immediately saw the body on the ground.

"We had nothin' to do with this," Elliot insisted. "Somebody's tryin' to frame us."

"Who is it?" Harlow asked Clint.

Clint leaned down and turned the body over.

"It's Larry," Clint said. "Somebody shoved a knife into his back."

"Maybe after he beat Harry Hayes to death?" Harlow asked.

"Well," Clint said, examining the body closer, "he's got blood on the front of his shirt. Doesn't look like his—at least, not from a knife in the back."

Clint stood up.

"Make a guess," Harlow said.

"Like you said, he beat Harry Hayes to death, then somebody shoved a knife into his back and dumped him here. We can look at the alley again, but I don't think we'll find his blood there."

"What if two men beat Harry to death, and then the other man killed this one?"

"Well," Clint said, "every time I've seen Larry, he's been with a man named Caleb. So, I figure now we have to find Caleb."

"We've checked all the saloons," Harlow said. "Now we just have to search the whole town."

"He worked for Teach," Clint said. "Maybe we should go and tell Mr. Teach that one of his men is dead."

"Why not?" Harlow asked.

\*\*\*

Clint and Harlow entered the Full House Saloon again. It looked even busier than before, as it was starting to get dark out and most of the businesses in town were closed.

They went to the bar and elbowed themselves some room. When the customers saw the badge, they moved grudgingly.

"You back again?" the bartender asked. "What now?"

"Have you seen Caleb?" Clint asked.

"Not lately."

"When did you last see Larry?"

"This mornin'," the bartender said.

"Was he with Caleb?"

"Yeah, they're always together."

"Not anymore," Harlow said.

"Whataya mean?"

"Larry's dead," Harlow said. "Somebody shoved a knife into his back."

"Probably a jealous husband or boyfriend," the bartender said. "That kid couldn't keep it in his pants."

"Do you know any husband or boyfriend in particular?" Harlow asked.

"Naw," the bartender said. "He got around."

"Is your boss in his office?" Harlow asked.

"No, he's upstairs."

"What's he doing?"

"He's got his woman up there with 'im," the bartender said. "Whataya think he's doin'?"

"Alma?" Clint asked.

"That's right."

Clint looked at Harlow.

"We've got to interrupt him."

"We catch 'im with his pants down, maybe we'll get somethin' from 'im," the sheriff said.

"Or we might get him mad, and he won't say a word." Clint looked at the bartender. "How's your boss going to react to the news that Larry's dead?"

"Who knows?" the bartender said. "He knows the kid's a wild one."

"And Caleb?" Clint asked.

"What about 'im?"

"Is he a wild one?"

"No," the bartender said. "He's older. He keeps his head."

Clint looked at Harlow.

"It's your call," Clint said. "Do we go up, or wait for him to come down?"

# Chapter Twenty-Three

Hiram Teach was pounding away at Alma Dodge when there was a knock on his door.

"What the hell—" he snapped.

"Don't answer it," Alma pleaded. "Keep goin'."

But he stood, sliding his cock from her hot pussy, so that it glistened with her juices.

"Goddamnit!" Alma swore. "I was almost there!"

"Shut up," he told her, pulling on his pants. "Just lie still and keep quiet."

She folded her arms across her full breasts and frowned.

Teach went to the door.

"Who is it?"

"Sheriff Harlow," a man's voice called, "and Clint Adams."

"Again?" Teach asked. He opened the door and stared at them. "What do you want now?"

"Sorry to interrupt you, Mr. Teach," Harlow said, "but we thought you'd be interested to know that your man, Larry, is dead."

"Dead? How?"

"Somebody stabbed him in the back," Clint said. "They dumped his body behind the Silver Blade Saloon."

"That hole?" Teach said. "Who would do that? And why?"

"We were hopin' you could tell us," Harlow said.

"Look," Teach said. "Thanks for bringing me the news, but I'm a little busy right now."

Over his shoulder they could see, the solidly built naked woman on the bed.

"We can see that," Clint said.

"Sheriff," Teach said, "why don't I come to your office in an hour, and we can talk?"

"That sounds good, Mr. Teach," Harlow said. "Maybe by then you can think of somethin' helpful."

"Yeah, maybe," Teach said.

"In an hour," Harlow said, and Teach closed the door in their faces.

Harlow turned to Clint.

"Whataya wanna do for an hour?"

"How about get something to eat?"

"Sounds good," Harlow said. They went downstairs and left the saloon.

***

"What was that about?" Alma asked, as Teach returned to the bed and sat down.

"One of my men was killed," Teach said. "The sheriff wants to talk to me about it."

"Now?"

Teach smiled and removed his pants.

"In an hour," he said, sliding back onto the bed with her.

She sighed as he mounted her and said, "I guess that'll have to do."

***

"I know that woman," Harlow said, as they left the saloon. "She's a local waitress."

"I've seen her around," Clint said.

"She works in a place you wouldn't eat at," the lawman told him. As they started walking away, Harlow said, "I'll have to be in my office when Teach gets there, so we better go and eat right now."

"The steak house?" Clint asked.

"Out of my league," Harlow said. "But you can eat there if you like. There's a small café I like."

"Sounds good to me," Clint said.

"This way," Harlow said, taking the lead.

\*\*\*

The café was called The Sunrise Café. Clint had not seen it before now.

"Sheriff!" the waiter said. "Good to see you. Your table's empty."

"Thanks, Al. This is my friend, he's gonna eat with me."

"Sure thing."

He walked them to the table and waited while they sat.

"Chili?" Al asked.

"You know it," Harlow said, then said to Clint, "Best chili in town."

"Sounds good to me."

"Right," the waiter said, "two chilis and . . . two beers?"

"Great," Clint said, and Harlow nodded to the man.

"Be back in a jiffy," Al said, and hurried to the kitchen.

"When Teach comes to your office, we're going to have to try and force him to give us Caleb. Otherwise, it'll take too long to find him."

"If he killed Harry Hayes and Larry, he may have left town."

"If he did that, it'll be like a confession," Clint pointed out.

Harlow nodded.

"I think Teach will give him up, and we'll get to talk to him."

"And he'll lie," the lawman said.

"Whether he did it or not," Clint said. "Do you know any of Teach's other men?"

"He brings them in and out of town when he needs them," Harlow said. "Most are money guns."

"Men who hire out their guns do their killing that way," Clint said. "No beatings, and no knives."

"So, we want Caleb, or somebody else like him," Harlow said.

They stopped talking when the waiter brought their meal and set their minds to eating.

# Chapter Twenty-Four

Sheriff Harlow and Clint Adams were both in the sheriff's office when Hiram Teach walked in.

"Both of you?" Teach asked.

"Mr. Adams has offered to help," Sheriff Harlow said. "I've accepted."

"Well," Teach said, "tell me what you've decided I can do for you."

"Bring your man Caleb in to talk to us," Harlow said.

"Why Caleb?"

"He was friends with Larry, wasn't he?" Clint asked.

"I suppose so," Teach said, "but that doesn't mean he knows who killed his friend."

"We just want to talk to him," Clint said. "He might have some ideas."

"Can you bring him in?" Harlow asked.

"I can bring him in," Teach said, "but I'll also come with him, if that's all right."

"It's fine with me," Harlow said.

"And any objection from Mr. Adams?" Teach asked.

"None."

"Where do you want to talk with him?" Teach asked.

"Right here would be fine," Harlow said.

"First thing in the morning?" Teach asked.

"That would be fine, too," Harlow said.

"We'll be here," Teach said. "I'll see you both then."

"Thank you, Mr. Teach," Harlow said.

The man turned and left.

"He's in a hurry to be cooperative," Clint said.

"So he is."

"Is he always like that?"

"I haven't had much to do with him, until now," Harlow said.

Clint thought if the sheriff had to act alone, he wouldn't have come this far. Having Clint to back him up was giving him more courage than usual.

"I guess we're done for the day," Clint said. "I'll meet you here first thing."

"Thanks for your help, Adams," Harlow said. "I guess you know I wouldn't be questioning Teach without you."

"I was just thinking that."

"Figured," Harlow said. "I ain't much of a lawman, you know."

"Maybe that's going to change."

***

When the knock came at Clint's door while he was reading Poe, he had a good idea who it was. Nevertheless, he went to answer with gun in hand.

"Who is it?"

"Holly."

He opened the door and let her in, then walked to the bedpost and holstered the gun.

"Were you expecting me?" she asked, removing her wrap.

"Let's say I'm not surprised. Have you eaten? I have nothing here to offer you."

"That's fine, I've had dinner. I'm not here to eat."

"I'm glad," he said.

"Not that either," she said, hurriedly. "I'm here to talk."

"Have a seat, then," he said. "Talk about what?"

"My father," she said, sitting in a chair. "You're supposed to be helping him."

"That's right."

"Then why did you and the sheriff question him like some criminal?"

"Nobody treated him like a criminal, Holly," Clint said. "A man was killed. We just wanted to know if your father knew anything."

"Why would he?"

"You never know what anyone knows until you ask."

"My father knows nothing about Harry Hayes being killed," she said. "It had to be some of Teach's men."

"Caleb and Larry," Clint said. "Except that Larry is now dead."

"Larry thought he was a fast gun."

"A fast gun can't do much against a knife in the back," Clint said.

"I can't stay, Clint," she said. "My father's waiting."

"Don't worry, Holly," Clint said. "I'd never try to make you choose between your father and me. I'd lose every time."

"Just help him," she said. "That's still all I really want."

"I'll do my best."

She went to the door and left.

*** 

Holly Clifford left the hotel, wishing she could have stayed in Clint Adams' bed. But her priority had to be her father, and not her carnal needs.

# Chapter Twenty-Five

Hiram Teach had sent for Caleb as soon as he left the sheriff's office and got back to the Full House. He was sitting at his table when the man arrived. From force of habit, Caleb grabbed two beers from the bar and carried them to the table.

"What's goin' on?" he asked his boss.

"The law and Clint Adams want to talk to you," Teach said.

"About Hayes, or Larry?"

"Probably both."

"And you want them to talk to me?"

"I promised to bring you in," Teach said.

"So they can arrest me?"

"So you can tell them you had nothing to do with killing Hayes and Larry."

"You think they're gonna believe me?"

"You'll make them believe you."

"And why's Harlow all of a sudden actin' like a real lawman?" Caleb asked.

"He's got Adams backing his play," Teach said, "but we're going to do something about that."

Tales of a Swamper

***

First thing in the morning Clint left the hotel and walked to the sheriff's office.

"Good morning," Harlow said, seated behind his desk.

" 'morning," Clint said.

"Did you have breakfast?" the lawman asked.

"No, I came right over," Clint said. "We can have breakfast after."

"That's what I figured," Harlow said. "Have a seat. I don't know how long we'll have to wait."

The door opened at that moment and Hiram Teach entered, leading a man Clint recognized.

"Not long, I guess," Clint said.

"Gentlemen," Teach said, "meet Caleb."

"The boss says you wanna talk to me," Caleb said. "What about?"

"I think you know," Harlow said.

"Try me."

"Somebody beat Harry Hayes to death in an alley," Harlow said. "Do you know anythin' about that?"

"No."

"What about Larry?" Clint said.

"What about him? He's a stupid kid."

109

"And a dead kid," Clint said. "Somebody stabbed him in the back."

"That's too bad."

"So you don't know anythin' about either death?" Harlow asked.

"Not a thing."

"When's the last time you saw Larry?" Clint asked.

"Lemme think," Caleb said. "Yesterday mornin'."

"Before or after you killed him?" Clint asked.

"There's no need to accuse him," Teach said. "He's here, ready to help you."

"He's lying through his teeth," Clint said.

Teach looked at Harlow.

"Sheriff, are you going to allow this man to accuse Caleb in this way?" Teach asked.

"I'm afraid that's what Mr. Adams thinks happened," Harlow said.

"And what do you think?" Teach asked.

"I'm still tryin' to make up my mind."

"Well," Teach said, "I don't think there's anything else we can do, so we'll be going."

"Don't leave town," Clint said. "Either of you."

"Why would we leave town?" Teach asked. "This is our home. Come on, Caleb."

Teach led Caleb from the office.

"Did you see the look on Caleb's face?" Clint asked. "What an arrogant sonofabitch."

"I was thinkin' that about Teach," Harlow said. "What do we do now?"

"I'm pretty sure Teach had Caleb and Larry kill Harry Hayes, and then Caleb killed Larry."

"Why kill his own man?" Harlow asked.

"He couldn't trust the kid to keep his mouth shut," Clint said.

"But he can trust Caleb?"

"To a certain extent."

"Adams," Harlow said, "Teach would never see me as a threat, but with you it's got to be different."

"I realize that," Clint said.

"So he'll send Caleb after you, next."

"I don't think so," Clint said.

"He won't try to kill you?" Harlow asked.

"He won't send Caleb after me," Clint said. "You said Teach has a lot of men."

"And, if need be, he can bring in more."

"Then that's what he'll do," Clint said. "He'll bring in somebody else to take care of me, maybe more than one."

# Chapter Twenty-Six

"Are you gonna just wait for them to come and get you?" Harlow asked, over breakfast at the café.

"Not exactly," Clint said. "You're going to pay attention to strangers riding into town."

"And you're gonna brace them as soon as they ride into town."

"I can't do that without making sure they're Teach's men," Clint explained.

"How you gonna do that?" Harlow asked.

"You watch for strangers," Clint said, "and I'll watch Teach."

"And Caleb?"

"Him, too, but I think when Teach brings in some guns, he's not going to need Caleb. In fact, he might even use his money guns to get rid of him."

"Why get rid of Caleb?" Harlow asked.

"Why get rid of Larry?" Clint asked. "He doesn't want anyone talking."

"How is any of this gonna keep Clifford from beating the mayor in the next election?" Harlow wondered.

"I get the feeling Teach is thinking about something else," Clint said.

"Like what?"

"I don't know," Clint said. "Maybe something to do with the railroad."

"He's got his nose in a lot of businesses," Harlow said. "It could be anythin'."

At that point the waiter came with their plates of ham-and-eggs and, since both of them were starving, they stopped talking and started eating.

\*\*\*

After breakfast they walked away from the café and started talking again.

"So what do you want me to do now?" Sheriff Harlow asked.

"Your job," Clint said. "Look for strangers."

"If they're Hiram Teach's men, they may not be strangers," Harlow said. "They may be men I've seen before."

"All right," Clint said, "then look for men you think might be money guns and point them out to me. I'll do the rest."

"You'll face them alone."

"I don't have anyone to watch my back," Clint said. "Unless you want the job."

"I told yo . . ."

"Yeah, I know," Clint said. "You're not much of a lawman."

"I'll keep an eye out," Harlow said, "that's about all I can do."

"But there's one more thing you can do."

"What's that?"

"Don't get killed."

That surprised Harlow. "You think they'd kill a lawman?"

"You said it yourself," Clint answered. "You're not much of a lawman."

\*\*\*

Harlow went back to his office, where Clint was sure he locked the door.

Clint went back to his hotel and found somebody waiting for him in the lobby.

"Mr. Clifford," he said.

"Mr. Adams."

"What brings you here?" Clint asked.

"Can we get a cup of coffee here?"

"Sure."

"And talk privately?"

"It's usually pretty empty here."

They walked to a table and sat. When the waiter came over Clint said, "Two coffees, please."

"Yes, Sir."

"What's on your mind, Mr. Clifford?"

"Two things," Clifford said. "Have you and the sheriff found out who killed Harry Hayes?"

"We have an idea."

"Teach," Clifford said. "That is, somebody working for Teach."

"Most likely."

"What are you going to do?"

"It's Teach who's going to do something," Clint said.

"Kill you?"

"Try to kill me," Clint said.

"Certainly not himself."

"No," Clint said, "he'll have someone try."

"But you're arrogant enough to think they won't be able to, eh?"

"If you want to call it that," Clint said, as the waiter set the coffee down.

Rather than pick it up and drink, Clifford simply stood up, preparing to leave.

"You said there were two things on your mind."

"That's right," Clifford said. "The other is my daughter."

"Holly? What about her?"

"Don't play with her feelings, Mr. Adams," Clifford said. "If you hurt my daughter, Hiram Teach won't have need to have you killed. I'll do it myself."

He turned and walked away.

# Chapter Twenty-Seven

Clint stepped into Holly's dress shop, the bell tinkling above his head. She came out of the back room, obviously expecting a customer. She smiled when she saw it was him.

"Wait," she said, "let me lock the door."

"Don't," he said. "I can't stay."

She stopped halfway to the door.

"Then why did you come?"

"I want to know what you told your father."

"About what?"

"About us," he said.

"Us? I didn't tell him anything. Why?"

"He came to my hotel and threatened to kill me."

"But you're supposed to be helping him," she said. "Why would he threaten to kill you?"

"Because of you."

"Oh, Clint," she said, shaking her head, "I would never tell my father anything about what we did."

"He said, if I did anything to hurt you, he'd kill me," Clint told her.

"Well, I'll have a talk with him and assure him that you've done nothing to hurt me. Besides, I doubt my father has ever killed anyone. I don't think he's capable of it. And he's definitely no match for you."

"You might as well talk him out of my thought of it," Clint said.

"I will. But what will you do now?"

"The only way I can see of ruining any plans Teach has is to prove he's behind both killings."

"But you said you thought that man Caleb killed Larry."

"Caleb works for Teach. That's what we have to prove."

"How do we do that?"

"That's my problem to figure out," Clint said. "I just want you to stay here till closing, then go home and calm your father down."

"I'll cook him his favorite dinner. That ought to do it," she predicted.

"Good," Clint said.

"But what will you do?"

"I'll talk to the sheriff, and see how long I can keep him acting like a real lawman."

"How's that going to work?"

"I need to help Sheriff Harlow find Caleb and turn him against Teach."

"Good luck with that," Holly said. "Harlow hasn't been a real sheriff in a long time."

Tales of a Swamper

\*\*\*

Hiram Teach met with two men in a back room of his saloon. One was Jesse Carver, a twenty-seven-year-old man who lived in a nearby town called Traderville. Carver considered himself the fastest gun alive.

The other man was forty-year-old Newly Fredericks, a man who lived in a house just outside of Firecreek.

Hiram Teach knew he could find men within fifty miles who considered themselves fast guns. Such men itched for an opportunity to prove themselves, and facing the Gunsmith would be such a chance. He also knew if these two men failed, there were plenty of others who considered themselves fast guns.

He heard Clint Adams had proved himself time and time again over the years. But, sooner or later, men like the Gunsmith, Wild Bill Hickok and Jesse James would come to an end at the point of a gun. He was hoping this would prove to be Clint Adams' time.

Carver and Fredericks eyed each other across the table, each with a cold beer in front of them. These two men considered themselves well known gunmen, yet neither had ever heard of the other.

"You're probably both wondering why I asked you here," Teach said.

"I'm wonderin' why he's here," Jesse Carver said. "Who is he?"

"This is Newly Fredericks," Teach said.

"Newly?" Carver asked, looking amused.

"You got a problem with my name?" Fredericks asked.

"I just ain't never heard of a name like that," Carver said, then added, "no offense."

"Enough of that," Teach said. "You're both here because you're big talkers. You both think you're the fastest gun alive. I'm going to give you each a chance to prove it."

"Against each other?" Fredericks asked.

"You want me to draw against this old man?" Carver asked.

"Who are you callin' an old man?" Fredericks demanded.

"That's enough," Teach snapped. "I've got another way for you to prove yourselves."

"And what might that be?" Fredericks asked.

"Clint Adams."

"The Gunsmith?" Carver asked. "He's even older than this old warhorse."

"I don't need this smart-mouthed kid to take care of Clint Adams," Fredericks told Teach.

"Now, listen good," Teach said. "Fighting each other will get you nothing. Killing the Gunsmith gets you everything."

"But what if I kill 'im before he does?" Carver asked, pointing at Fredericks.

"If the Gunsmith gets killed, I'll pay you both."

"Even if I do it without him?" Carver asked.

"That's right, so you see, competing gets you nothing."

"This don't sound fair," Carver said.

"You don't know it, kid," Fredericks said, "but this setup saves your life."

"Why you—" Carver started but Teach cut him off.

"Once the Gunsmith is dead, you two can do whatever you want. Put up the money I pay you both and go head-to-head for it."

"That ain't a bad idea," Carver said.

"We work together, kill Clint Adams, and then go against each other, winner take all. I like it."

Teach stood up and said, "Then get to it."

"Whoa, wait a second," Fredericks said. "How much are we gettin' paid?"

"Believe me," Teach said, "it'll be a lot."

# Chapter Twenty-Eight

When Clint left Holly's dress shop, he went directly to the sheriff's office.

"I was hoping you'd show up," Harlow said, from his seat behind his desk. There was a coffee mug on the desk, but no smell of coffee in the room.

"Something happen?" Clint asked.

"Two strangers rode into town," the lawman said. "They went right to Teach's saloon."

"A lot of strangers stop in a saloon when they hit town," Clint said. "Did they look like drifters? Cowboys?"

"Guns," Harlow said. "They were both wearing pistols in holsters.

"Did they ride in together?"

"No," Harlow said, "about an hour apart."

"And the first man was still in the saloon when the second man went in?"

"Oh, yeah."

"Then one of us should check them out."

"One of us?"

"You," Clint said. "You're the law."

"We've been through this—"

"You're wearing a badge," Clint said. "If these men were brought in to kill me, they won't lift a finger against you. Teach wouldn't stand for it."

"And if they're just passin' through, and one of them wanted to kill a lawman?"

"Teach still wouldn't stand for it," Clint said. "You don't have to brace them, just walk in, have a drink and keep your ears open."

"And if I don't hear anything helpful?"

"Just walk right out again, and we'll figure something else out.

Harlow reluctantly got to his feet.

"I'll wait here," Clint said.

"Sure thing," Harlow said.

"Don't worry," Clint said, "if I hear shooting, I'll come running."

"Yeah," Harlow said, "you'll be in time to help pick me up off the floor."

"Don't worry, Sheriff," Clint said, "it's all going to go fine."

As Harlow left the office, Clint gave him credit for going to the Full House Saloon even though he was afraid.

And he knew he would feel like shit if he was wrong, and Harlow ended up dead.

***

When Sheriff Harlow entered the Full House Saloon his heart was racing, and his mouth was dry. He walked to the bar and waved the bartender over.

"Cold beer," he said.

"Comin' up, Sheriff."

When the bartender set the beer in front of him, he asked, "Where's the boss?"

The bartender shrugged and said, "I ain't sure."

"What about the two strangers who came in here earlier?" Harlow asked.

"Strangers?"

"They came in an hour apart," the lawman said. "I don't see them now."

"They probably came and went," the bartender said.

"And you didn't see them?"

"I been busy," the bartender said. "As you can see, we're crowded."

Harlow drank his beer down but found that his mouth was still dry. He had gone as far as he could with this.

"Okay," he said to the barkeep, "okay." He dug a coin out of his pocket.

"On the house, Sheriff."

Harlow hesitated, then said, "Thanks," and walked out, expecting a bullet in the back.

# Chapter Twenty-Nine

"How did it go?" Clint asked, as Harlow re-entered his office.

"Not well," the lawman said, "but I'm alive. I talked to the bartender, but he gave me nothin'."

"Then maybe it's time for me to get a drink."

"If those two men were brought in to take care of you, it'll be two-to-one."

"Do you want to back me?" Clint asked.

"I wouldn't be much good to you."

"Then I'll take the two-to-one odds," Clint said.

"It's gettin' late," Harlow said. "That saloon will be packed."

"They won't all be against me," Clint said. "I'll take the chance."

"You'll need help," Harlow said.

"Do you know anyone in town who might back my play?" Clint asked.

"No one," Harlow said. "Teach has collected the gunmen in town, at one time or another. The others are storekeepers and cowhands."

"Then I'll go it alone."

"Good luck," Harlow said, as Clint left the office.

\*\*\*

When Holly got home that night, she immediately challenged her father.

"What's wrong with you, father?"

Ben Clifford looked up from packing his pipe.

"That's not the way you should talk to your father," he said.

"It is when he's been acting like a bloody fool," she said.

"What's on your mind, daughter?"

"Why the hell would you threaten to kill Clint Adams when he's trying to help you?"

"I simply told him what I'd do if he hurt you," Clifford said.

"If he's helping you, what makes you think he'd hurt me?" Holly asked.

"Because of the kind of man he is."

"Right now, he seems like the kind of man who's helping you."

"Yes, but why?" he asked.

"What's it matter why?" she asked.

"Holly," he said, lighting his pipe, "nobody does something for nothing. I don't want you to be the foolish one."

"I trust Clint," she said.

127

"Then you're already being foolish," Clifford said. "Are you making dinner tonight?"

"Ooh, you!" she snapped, and went into the kitchen.

\*\*\*

Clint approached the Full House Saloon as darkness fell. Light and noise came from the inside. As he entered, he also felt the heat thrown off from all the bodies. As he looked around, he saw no empty tables. There were a couple of girls, dressed in blue and green, working the floor.

When he walked to the bar, he had to elbow himself a place. He wondered if any of the men standing there were one of the two strangers.

"Beer," he told the bartender.

"Comin' up."

The bartender set a beer down in front of him, then left and walked to the back room. Clint assumed he was telling Hiram Teach that he was there . . .

\*\*\*

Teach looked up from his seat at the table when the bartender entered.

"He's here."

"That's all," Teach told the man.

As the bartender left, the other two men continued to eat their meal.

"Stop eating," Teach said.

Jesse Carver and Newly Fredericks looked at each other, and then set down their utensils. Teach picked his up and started eating his stew again.

"This is a stroke of luck," he said to them. "The Gunsmith walked right into my saloon."

"You want us to kill him now?" Carver asked.

"In a crowded saloon?" Fredericks added.

"I hired you to kill him," Teach said. "When and how you do it is your business. But he's here now, so you can do *something*. Like get to know him."

Carver laughed.

"You mean make friends?" he asked.

"He means take a look at him," Fredericks said. "Study him. Figure him out."

Teach decided at that moment that Fredericks was the smarter of the two.

***

Carver and Fredericks stepped from the backroom and stopped just outside the doorway.

"How do we want to play this?" Carver asked.

Fredericks was pleased that the younger man was asking his opinion.

"Let's keep some distance between us," he said. "I know his reputation, but he's only got one gun. This way, one of us will get 'im."

"Yeah," Carver said, "but he'll get one of us."

"That may be."

"I don't like the sound of that," the younger man said.

"Okay, then let's use this time to feel him out," Fredericks suggested. "Let's see how far he's willin' to go."

"What if he goes for his gun?" Carver asked.

"His reputation says he won't," Fredericks said. "Not first, anyway."

"If you're gonna count on that part of his reputation," Carver asked, "what about the part that says he's the fastest gun alive?"

"I guess we're gonna find out," Fredericks said.

# Chapter Thirty

Clint saw the two men step out of the backroom soon after the bartender returned to the bar. The saloon was packed with people, but Clint only had eyes for those two men, and they for him.

He watched the two men split up and go separate ways. He knew their intention was to keep space between them. Not that it mattered as long as there were so many people between them.

Carver and Fredericks kept moving apart, and then started walking toward Clint. He noticed the bartender also watching them, with his hand beneath the bar.

"You bring a shotgun out from under there and you'll be the first one to eat a bullet."

The bartender jerked his hand from under the bar as if it had been burned.

Little-by-little the men standing near Clint began to understand that something was brewing, and slowly moved away from him. Before long, Carver and Fredericks had a clear sight line to Clint, still standing at the bar.

Then it got quiet. All of the people in the saloon had moved to one side or the other. leaving a clear line between Carver and Fredericks, and Clint.

"Well," Clint said, "I came here with a question in mind. I guess I got my answer."

"What was that?" Fredericks asked.

"Were you two men here for me? I guess you are."

"We just wanted to get a look at you, Adams," Carver said.

"We might as well introduce ourselves," Clint said. "You know who I am."

"My name's Jesse Carver," the younger man said.

"Newly Fredericks," the older man said.

"I never heard of either one of you," Clint admitted.

"We don't have the reputation you do, Adams," Fredericks said.

"But we're fast," Carver said. "At least, I am. Wanna see?"

"Carver, don't!" Fredericks yelled, but he was too late.

Clint didn't know Carver, so he didn't know if the younger man was going to do some trick shooting, or if he was making his move. So he had no choice. He drew his gun and fired. His bullet struck Carver in the chest, before the man was able to clear leather.

132

As quiet as the room had been, it seemed even quieter after Clint's shot.

"Jesus," somebody breathed.

"Fredericks—" Clint asked, holstering his gun.

"Not right now, Adams," Fredericks said. "I'm not as big a fool as the kid was. Like you said, I just wanted to get introduced—and I guess we did."

From the back of the room Hiram Teach said, "All right, that's enough. You men get back to your drinking and gambling. Except for a few of you. Pick up that man and take him to the undertaker."

Several men bent to the task and carried Jesse Carver from the saloon.

Teach walked to the bar, where he joined Clint and Fredericks.

"Give each of these men a drink on the house," he told the bartender. "And pour one for me."

"Yes, Sir."

When they all had a drink, Teach said to Clint, "That was the fastest thing I've ever seen."

"Same here," Fredericks said. He tossed down his drink, looked at Teach and said, "Thanks for the whiskey. So long."

Clint and Teach watched the man walk out.

"What are you going to do now, Teach?" Clint asked. "Both your guns are gone."

"I don't know what you mean, Adams," Teach said. "I don't like this sort of thing in my place. I'd appreciate it if you wouldn't come in here again. I get the feeling you bring this sort of thing with you."

He put his glass down, walked to his office door and went in.

\*\*\*

Clint watched Teach walk into his office, then looked at the bartender.

"That was somethin'," the bartender said.

"Yeah, but probably not what your boss wanted."

"I dunno what ya mean," the man said. "Want another drink?"

"No, thanks," Clint said. "I'll be on my way before somebody else gets brave."

\*\*\*

In his office, Teach slammed the door behind him, angrily.

Fredericks had every chance against Adams when Carver made his move. The older man could have drawn and fired, but was obviously shocked by Clint Adams' move, and preferred to leave the saloon alive.

Teach was going to have to find men of a totally different quality.

# Chapter Thirty-One

When Clint returned to the sheriff's office, Harlow looked up from his desk in surprise.

"Back already?" he asked. "What happened?"

"I found both strangers," Clint said. "I had to kill one, but the other ran."

"He ran?"

"After he saw me outdraw his friend," Clint said.

"Do you know who they were?"

"I don't."

"Was Teach there?"

"Yes," Clint said. "He bought me a drink."

"Why?"

"He was trying to convince me he wasn't involved with those two men."

"And he didn't succeed?"

"No, he didn't," Clint said. "I think now he needs more competent gunmen. That'll take him a while."

"So what do we do in the meantime?" Harlow asked.

"Figure something out," Clint said.

Harlow sat back in his chair.

"How long do you intend to stay here in Firecreek?" he asked.

"I've already been here longer than I thought I would," Clint said. "I made the mistake of getting to know Harry Hayes. Now I want to take care of those who killed him."

"That'd be Larry and Caleb. Larry's already dead."

"I want who was behind Harry's murder. That would seem to be Teach."

"So you'll be here until you can kill Teach?" Harlow asked.

"I'd rather see him in jail, and I've agreed to help Ben Clifford all I can."

"Yeah, but help him what? Become mayor?" the lawman asked.

"I suppose I promised to keep him alive to move ahead with his plans."

"Plans for what?"

"I don't know," Clint said. "He hasn't told me that."

"Do you think he will?"

Clint shrugged.

"I don't get it, Adams," Harlow said. "Why not just saddle up and ride out?"

"That's a very good question," Clint admitted.

***

"You're Angry," Alma said, rolling over.

"Things haven't gone the way I planned," he told her, sitting on the edge of the bed. "I took it out on you. I'm sorry."

"That's all right," she said. "That's what I'm here for, isn't it?"

He looked at her over his shoulder.

"No, it's not."

"Is this about the shooting?" she asked.

"Yes," he said, "that's what didn't go as I planned."

"So what will you do?"

He shrugged.

"Make a new plan."

"Soon?"

"It will have to be soon," he said. "The railroad people are coming to town next week."

"Who knows that?"

"Those of us on the town council."

"What about the Gunsmith?"

He turned and looked at her.

"What do you know about him?"

"Just what I've heard," she said. "That he's in town. Is he part of your plan, or part of your problem?"

He looked away from her and said, "I'm afraid he's both."

# Chapter Thirty-Two

Clint did some serious thinking in his room that night. Perhaps the smartest thing for him to do would be to ride out. Hiram Teach was bound to bring in a few more gunmen each time someone failed to kill him. Why wait? He could leave the town to its own problems. The only thing was, he felt he owed something to Harry Hayes and, to a lesser extent, Holly Clifford.

Before he turned in, he decided he was committed to staying in Firecreek at least until he had dealt with Teach for having Harry Hayes killed. The old swamper deserved better than to be beaten to death, and Clint felt he was the only man who was going to get it for him.

*** 

In the morning, Clint woke with a plan. It was something he had mentioned to Sheriff Harlow in passing, but now he figured it was his best bet. He wanted to find Caleb and turn him against Teach. He was certain that Caleb was one of two men who killed Harry Hayes, the other being Larry. And it was likely that Teach had then had Caleb kill Larry. Caleb would never confess to two murders. But if he thought Teach was planning to have him killed, he might help Clint put Teach away.

Clint had to find Caleb and let himself be seen talking with him. That would get back to Teach. He needed to get Caleb to suspect Teach, and Teach to suspect Caleb. Of course, he didn't know what kind of relationship the two men had. If it was simply employer/employee, then his plan was possible. But if the two men were truly friends, it might be harder.

He wanted to propose his plan to Sheriff Harlow.

\*\*\*

Clint and Harlow spoke on the front porch of the hotel, in plain sight of the entire town.

"I don't know of anyone who claims to be friends with Hiram Teach," Harlow said. "I don't think you're gonna have to overcome any feelings of friendship between them."

"Then all I need to do is find Caleb," Clint said.

"That might be difficult, since he seems to have dropped out of sight."

"Has he left town?"

"That I don't know."

"And as for Teach, he has *no* friends?"

"He's on the Town Council, but I don't know of any of those men who would claim him as a friend."

"That's too bad," Clint said. "We could use somebody."

They sat side-by-side in silence for a few moments before Harlow spoke.

"There is one person who's close to him."

Clint looked at the lawman.

"The waitress?" he asked.

Harlow nodded.

"Yes, Alma."

"Where does she work?" Clint asked.

"At the Wallflower Café," Harlow said. "The food's bad, which is why I feed it to the prisoners."

Clint laughed.

"Is she in love with him?" he asked.

"That I don't know," Harlow said, "but they spend a lot of time together in his room."

"So there's no doubt about what they're doing," Clint said.

"I don't think so."

"Then I guess maybe it's time for me to meet Alma," Clint said.

"You'll have to go to the café," Harlow said, standing.

"I'll have lunch there today," Clint said.

"Don't have anythin' more complicated than a sandwich," Harlow warned him.

"Thanks for the warning."

\*\*\*

At lunchtime Clint went to the café and got a table. It was Alma who seated him.

"Do ya wanna see a menu?" she asked.

"I think I'll just have a chicken sandwich," Clint said.

"That's probably a good idea," she said. "Coffee?"

"Yes, please."

When she returned with his coffee, he took a good look at her. In her forties, she had obviously been a beauty in her youth. Now she wore the weight of hard years on her face, but her body was still good. Clint thought that when she smiled, she probably took some of the lines out of her face and made herself almost pretty.

There weren't many people eating in the place, probably because of the quality of the food. When she brought him his sandwich he asked, "Can you sit a while?"

She looked around and said, "Probably. The rush hasn't started yet."

She sat across from him.

"Is there generally a lunch rush?" he asked.

"No," she said, "I was joking."

"Most people smile when they make a joke," Clint told her.

"There's not very much to smile about around here," she replied.

# Chapter Thirty-Three

"What do you want from me, Mr. Adams?"

"You know who I am?" he asked.

"By this time everyone in town knows who you are," she told him. "Once you got off the hotel porch and started movin' around, the word got out."

"Word got out," he asked, "or Hiram Teach told you?"

"Of course, Hiram knew first," Alma said. "He knows everythin'."

"Does he know who killed Harry Hayes and that young fella, Larry?"

"I don't know anythin about murder."

"But Teach does, is that what you're sayin'?"

"I'm not sayin' nothin'," she said.

"What do you know about Teach's business?"

"He owns The Full House Saloon."

"And his other businesses?"

"He owns the freight company," she said.

"And?"

"And some other businesses I don't know nothin' about," she said.

She wasn't telling him much, but she also wasn't standing up and walking away. He bit into his sandwich and found it dry."

"You want some butter for that?" she asked.

"It would help," he said.

She went to the kitchen, came back with a stick of butter and spread some on the sandwich for him.

"I don't know if that'll help," she said.

He bit into it and chewed.

"Not much," he admitted.

"Well," she said, "you didn't come here to eat, you came here to talk to me."

Since she knew that, he dropped the sandwich back onto the dish and ignored it.

"Why do you think I wanted to talk to you?"

"Well, it could be because you saw me in the saloon, and you think I'd be good in bed. You'd be right, I am very good."

"I don't doubt it."

"Would you like to find out for yourself?" she asked. "I could close up and we could go into the backroom."

"I thought you were Teach's girl."

"I spend time with Hiram," she said, "but he doesn't own me. And I haven't been a girl for a very long time."

"I see."

144

She stood up, put her hands on her hips and thrust her chest out at him.

"Whata you say? I've got the time."

"You're serious?"

"Dead serious," she said. "I've heard of your reputations with guns and women. You already proved yourself with a gun. How about proving yourself with me?"

"Why would you do that? You don't even know me."

"I like sex," she said. "And I'm curious. I'm gonna lock up. Wait here."

She went to the front door and, in spite of himself, he waited. He found he was also curious.

\*\*\*

Sheriff Harlow was across the street, curious about what Clint Adams might find out from Alma. When he saw the shade drawn on the door and the OPEN sign turned to CLOSED. He figured Adams was going to be in there for some time, and would probably learn more than he bargained for.

He turned and started back to his office.

\*\*\*

She came back across the room, put her hand out to Clint and said, "Let's go."

"Where's your boss?" he asked, standing up.

"He don't come in til suppertime," she said. "Until then, I'm the cook and the waitress. That's part of the reason the food's so bad. I'm a terrible cook."

She walked him through a doorway and into a back room. He almost expected to find a bed there, but there was a lot of room filled with barrels and cartons.

"Wait," she said, "there are some blankets back here."

She released his hand, walked over to some cartons and brought a few blankets from behind them. She spread them on the floor and stepped back.

"There, that should do it."

She turned to face him and removed her apron.

"I'm not as young as I used to be, and my face— well, I think you'll like the rest."

She was wearing a simple cotton dress, which she unbuttoned in the back and peeled off. She wore nothing underneath.

"There," she said, tossing the dress aside and spreading her arms. "I think my body has held up pretty well, don't you?"

She had full breasts and hips, solid legs from years of waiting tables. Turning for him, she showed him her lovely, chunky butt.

"Your turn," she said.

# Chapter Thirty-Four

As she stood there naked in front of him, it occurred to Clint that this might be her way of getting his gun off of him. The front door was locked. There was a back door, so he walked to it and checked. It was also locked.

"Are you afraid we'll be interrupted?" she asked. "We won't."

He looked at her again. She was the definition of sex. Her dark nipples were already swollen, and she was wet between her legs.

"I'm ready when you are, Mr. Adams," she said. "If you think I'm tryin' to get your gun, then get naked and keep it on. I don't mind."

The room was filled with the smell of her, and he started to undress. He took off his boots, set them aside, then unstrapped his holster and put it within easy reach. After that, he removed the rest of his clothes. He now stood naked, his hard cock poking at the air, as if it was trying to get at her.

"My God," she said, staring, "this is gonna be so damn good."

He stepped onto the blankets, and she fell to her knees in front of him. At first, she simply cradled his cock and balls, enjoying the feel of them in her hands. Then she closed one hand around him and began to stroke him. She did this until he grew to his full length and was almost painfully hard. That was when she opened her mouth and did her best to take as much of him in as she could. She suckled him until he was drenched with her saliva, then dropped down onto her back, pulling him with her. He knew what she wanted and he gave it to her. He slid into her wet pussy until he was fully sunk in, then began to move in and out of her, never pulling fully out before ramming himself in again.

"Oh, yes," she began to gasp aloud, "oh my, yes . . . more . . . more . . ."

He gave her more and more and kept giving it to her until her entire body stiffened beneath, and then was rocked by wave after wave of pleasure, causing her to close her arms and thighs around him.

"Come on," she cried out, "do it, give it to me, let go . . ."

He let go and exploded inside of her with such force that they both cried out, and he wondered if anyone passing by outside could hear them . . .

\*\*\*

They rolled around on the blanket, and she managed to climb atop him and take him inside again.

"Aren't you worried about customers coming to the door?" he asked.

"I don't care if they never come," she said, dangling her full breasts in his face. He took the nipples in to his mouth in turn and sucked them. The woman had an amazing body, and the more time he spent with her the more the years seemed to fade from her face. At one point, while she rode him hard, the look of pleasure on her face almost made her beautiful as she must have once been. She was so good at what she was doing, and seemed to be in such command of her body that her insides were gripping and milking him.

As he exploded into her again, he couldn't help wondering if she had always been a waitress, or if she had once made her way in another trade . . .

***

"Never," she said, as they dressed.

"Never what?" he asked.

"There was a moment there when you wondered if I had ever been a whore," she said. "The answer is, never."

"Alma—"

"I'm simply a woman who likes sex and is very good at it," she told him.

"I can't argue with that."

As he strapped his gun back on, she said, "And see? No one tried to break in and kill you. If someone in town wants you dead, they'll have to do it without me."

"I'm glad to hear it."

"Come into the café and I'll give you some bad coffee," she said, and he followed her through the doorway.

\*\*\*

While he drank coffee, she was in the kitchen preparing for what passed as a lunch or supper rush, no one else came through the door.

Eventually, she came out of the kitchen and said, "My boss is here, and he's taken over the cookin'."

"Is he good at it?"

"Better than me," she said, "but I wouldn't recommend you try."

# Chapter Thirty-Five

Clint had enjoyed the two hours he spent with Alma in the back room, but he came out of the café knowing nothing new about Hiram Teach. He suspected she'd had sex with him to keep him otherwise occupied.

When he entered his hotel, he found Sheriff Harlow waiting in the lobby for him.

"I was wonderin' how long you'd take," the lawman said.

"Come on up to my room," Clint said.

The sheriff followed him. They didn't speak until the door was closed and locked.

"What happened?" Harlow asked. "What'd you find out?"

"About Teach? Nothing."

"Then . . .oh."

"Yeah," Clint said, "she took off her dress and I forgot all about him."

"Did she say anythin' about Caleb?"

"We never even talked about him."

"She's that good?" the lawman asked.

"Better," Clint said. "She pretty much made a fool out of me. She's quite a woman."

"Do you think Teach had her do that?"

"I think she's smart enough to do it on her own."

"Or she was just curious."

Clint laughed.

"That's what she said."

"I don't know what that's like," Harlow said. "Women aren't curious about me."

"Maybe you're lucky."

"So what will you do now?"

"I'll walk around town and look for Caleb. Maybe I'll get lucky and come across him."

"Somebody might take a shot at you."

"Yes," Clint said, "they might."

Harlow hesitated, then stammered, "Look, I can't— I mean, I couldn't—"

"Relax," Clint said, "I don't expect you to watch my back. Just watch your own."

Harlow nodded, turned and left the room.

***

"Zeb," Alma said to her boss in the kitchen, "I have to go out."

The fat cook looked at her and said, "We got any customers?"

"None."

"So go."

"I'll be back," she told him.

He looked bored.

Alma left the café and rushed to The Full House Saloon.

\*\*\*

Teach was in his office when somebody knocked on the door.

"Come!" he said.

The door opened and Alma came in.

"What are you doin' here?" Teach asked. "You're not supposed to come until tonight."

"I had to see you."

"Close the door!"

She did so.

"What is it?"

"The Gunsmith came to see me today."

Teach laughed shortly.

"Clint Adams came to eat in your café?"

"No, I said he came to see me."

"Why?"

"To ask about you."

"What did you tell him?"

"Nothing," she said. "I said I knew you owned this place, and that was it."

Teach sat back in his chair.

"Why would he come to see you?" he wondered.

"He saw me here the other day," she said. "And everyone knows that we . . . spend time together."

"*Everyone* knows?"

"Well," she said, "a lot of people do."

Teach didn't like that.

"Maybe we should take a break," he said.

"You got somebody else in mind?"

"No."

"Because if you wanna fuck somebody else, just say so," she said. "But you ain't ever gonna find anybody better than me."

"You don't think so?"

"Somebody younger, maybe," she went on, "but nobody better."

He hesitated, then said, "Yeah, okay."

"Am I still comin' by tonight?" she asked.

Teach studied her for a long moment, and then said, "Yeah, come by."

"I'll see you tonight," she said, and left.

Teach sat back in his chair, made a steeple out of his hands, and did some thinking.

# Chapter Thirty-Six

Clint left the hotel and began his walk around town, keeping an eye out for Caleb. He didn't bother with The Full House Saloon. He doubted Teach would allow Caleb to be seen in there.

There were other saloons and cafés in town. He looked in all of them with no luck. It seemed obvious that the man was either hiding out or had left town. For this reason, he checked the livery stables. He wanted to see if the man was hiding in any of them. He also wanted to find out where Caleb kept his horse, and if it was still there.

"Yeah," the hostler at one of them said, "He keeps his sorrel here."

"Is it here now?"

"It was the last time I looked," the old hostler said, concentrating on his whittling.

"Well, look again."

He looked up from his block of wood, stared into Clint's eyes, then put the wood down and went inside. When he came out, he picked up his wood.

"It's still there," he said.

"Thanks for looking," Clint said, and moved on.

Tales of a Swamper

***

By late afternoon he had found no trace of Caleb in town. The fact that his horse was in its stall did not necessarily mean he hadn't left town. He could have gone on foot or used another horse.

If he was going to try to find friends of Caleb's and question them, that would mean going to the Full House Saloon. If he did that, he was very likely to run into Teach. He decided to stop in there and make a point of seeing Teach.

As he entered, an eerie quiet came over the crowded room. Alma was right, everyone in town knew who he was, especially after he'd had to kill Carver.

"Whataya have?" the bartender asked.

"A beer, and your boss."

"I can give ya a beer," the barman said, "the boss is in his office. But he don't like bein' disturbed."

"I'll take my chances," Clint said.

"Then here ya go," the man said, setting a beer down.

"Thanks," Clint said, "I'll take it with me. What's your boss drink?"

"He's got his own," the bartender said.

Clint walked across the room with his beer, aware that he was being watched by almost everyone in the room. He was also aware that any of these men could suddenly decide to get brave.

When he knocked on Teach's office door the man called out, "Come!" He entered.

Teach was seated behind his desk.

"Mr. Adams," he said. "Come in, what can I do for you?"

Clint entered the room and closed the door behind him.

"I'm looking for Caleb, Mr. Teach," Clint said. "I was wondering if you know where he is."

"Why would I know?"

"He's your man," Clint said.

"Why do you want him?"

"I want to talk to him about the killing of Harry Hayes."

"Why do you care about the killing of that old swamper?" Teach asked.

"I liked the old swamper," Clint said.

"And you think Caleb killed him?"

"Or he knows who did," Clint said. "You lost another man, Larry. Maybe he knows about that, too."

"Caleb's not a murderer."

"I'd still like to talk to him," Clint said. "He might have something to tell me."

"Why isn't the sheriff doing this?" Teach asked.

"You know the answer to that better than I do," Clint said, and left.

\*\*\*

Clint went to the Jack of Spades Saloon, which was only slightly less busy than The Full House.

"Ain't seen you sittin' across the street in a while," the bartender, Race Gentry, said.

"I've been busy," Clint replied.

"What'll you have?"

"Beer."

Gentry put it in front of him, then didn't move.

"What've ya been busy with?"

"Finding out who killed Harry Hayes."

"Oh, that."

"You got any ideas? He worked for you."

"He worked for everyone in town at one time or another," Gentry said. "He could've got anybody mad at him."

"Mad enough to kill him?"

"I wouldn't have thought so," Gentry said, "but you never know."

A customer at the other end of the bar called for Gentry, who went down and tended to him, then returned.

"I've been looking for Caleb Tarr."

"You think Caleb killed Harry?"

"I do," Clint said. "And probably Larry."

"Larry was no loss," Gentry said. "He was a stupid kid."

"So you think Caleb did it?"

"That I don't know," Gentry said. "I just know Larry was no loss."

"And what do you know about Hiram Teach?"

"He thinks he's the top man in town," Gentry said.

"And you don't agree?"

"I don't see any reason not to let him think so," Gentry said.

"Are you friends?"

"He has no friends that I know of," Gentry said, "but we're both business owners and we're both on the Town Council."

"What can you tell me about him?"

"I've already told you all I know," Gentry said. "Sometimes he has a drink here, sometimes I have one there. That's it." The batwings opened and four men entered. "I've got customers."

"Right," Clint said. "Thanks."

He finished his beer and left the saloon, wondering if he could get more out of Race Gentry when he wasn't so busy.

# Chapter Thirty-Seven

Clint assumed Caleb would be told he was looking for him, either by someone in town, or by Teach. For that reason, he thought he should stakeout the livery where Caleb's horse was.

"You wanna sleep in here?" the older liveryman asked. "Ain't you got a hotel room?"

"I do."

"Then why you wanna—oh, wait. You're still lookin' for that fella, Caleb?"

"Yes."

"So you think he'll try to get his horse when it gets dark?"

"I'm hoping he will," Clint said. "And if anyone tells him I'm waiting, I wouldn't like it, at all." He gave the man a hard look.

"Hey," the old man said, "I ain't gonna say nothin' to nobody." He put his hand in his pocket. "Here's the key. You can just leave it on the desk when you're done."

"Thanks," Clint said, accepting it. "Where will you be?"

"I don't sleep here," the man said. "I got a small house just outside of town."

"Okay," Clint said. "I'll be back after dark."

"Any time you want," the old man said. "You got the key. I won't be back til six a.m."

"Hopefully," Clint said. "I'll be gone by then."

"And if he don't come?"

"I'll try again the next night."

"Yeah, but what if he—"

"What's your name, Pop?"

"Pat."

"Don't worry about it, Pat. I'll do the worrying."

"Yeah, okay."

Clint left the livery. He had several hours before dark. The plan would be a bust if Caleb had another horse, or left town on foot.

***

Hiram Teach opened the back door of the Full House Saloon and let Caleb in.

"I'm tired of hidin' out," Caleb said.

"That's why I'm paying you now, so you can go," Teach said, handing the man some money."

Caleb started to count it, but Teach pushed his hands down.

"Don't count it here," he said. "I gave you something extra."

"Thanks, boss."

"Get out of town tonight."

"When can I come back?"

"Not til after the election," Teach told him, "or we resolve the railroad question."

"Or when I hear he's dead," Caleb said, meaning the Gunsmith.

"Yeah, that, too."

Caleb started to leave, then turned and asked, "You think I should take my own horse?"

"It's a good animal, isn't it?"

"Best I ever had."

"Well, you'll need a good horse, so take it."

"What if Adams tracks me?"

"Don't worry," Teach said, "I'll make sure he doesn't."

"Okay, boss," Caleb said. "I'll see ya."

Teach nodded and slapped the man on the back. He hoped he was right that Clint Adams was smart enough to be staking out the livery where Caleb left his horse. After tonight, the only problem he should have to deal with was Clint Adams, himself, and he had already sent for the men who would take care of that little matter.

# Chapter Thirty-Eight

Clint planned on spending the night in the livery if Caleb didn't show up. He had pretty much looked everywhere he could in town during the day, and no one seemed to know exactly where Caleb lived. If Caleb didn't come tonight, he would do it again the next night. If that didn't work, he would have to figure out a way to push Hiram Teach into a mistake.

His own horse, Toby, was in another livery and he checked on him before he went to Pat's livery. He made himself a comfortable corner on some hay in one of the stalls and settled in to wait.

\*\*\*

Hiram Teach fucked Alma as hard and fast as he could, then rolled away.

"Is that all?" she asked, rolling onto her back.

"Go to sleep," he said, "I'll wake you if I need you again."

"Whatever you say, Hiram," she said, pulling the sheet up over her.

"I'm going to my office," he said, dressing. "I'll be back later."

Alma was already snoring when he left the room.

\*\*\*

Seated behind his desk, in his office, Teach wrote out three telegrams that he would send the next day. Each of the men he was sending them to charged a large fee for their services. Teach was not prepared to pay for their services on his own. He was going to have to approach Race Gentry and a few of the other Town Council members, to pay their share. Hiring these men was the only way he could see of getting rid of Clint Adams for good. The man was determined to be a thorn in his side. As such, Adams would be in the way when it came to taking Firecreek in the direction Teach wanted the town to go.

If he couldn't kill the Gunsmith, he would have to go a step further, but killing Ben Clifford was not something he wanted to do. If it was the only way to keep him from becoming mayor, he would have no choice. And, of course, the ideal way to go would be to get rid of both Clifford and Adams. Such a venture would take the right kind of men and the right amount of them.

He finished the telegrams and put them in the top drawer of his desk. In the morning he would send them, and then go and see Gentry and the others, but separately, not in a council meeting.

He blew out his lamp and left the office to go back to his room.

*** 

When a door opened in the livery, Clint was immediately alerted. He sat up and stared into the darkness. It was hard to see, but he looked in the direction of Caleb's horse and saw a dark figure moving. He shifted over to an oil lamp hanging from a post. Very quickly he struck a Lucifer match and lit the lamp, which flooded the area with light. Caleb froze in place and stared at the lamp then Clint.

"Hello, Caleb," he said.

Quickly, Caleb said, "You ain't gonna kill me, are ya?"

"Not if you don't go for that gun on your hip," Clint told him.

Caleb swiftly raised his hands as far from the gun as possible.

"Why don't you just take the gun from your holster with two fingers and toss it away. Then we can talk."

Caleb did as he was told.

"Do the same with the knife."

Caleb obeyed.

"Now sit over there on a bale of hay."

Caleb walked over and sat, his hands still in the sir.

"Put your hands down."

Caleb did.

"How'd you know I'd be here?" he asked.

Instead of telling him the truth, that it was a hunch, Clint lied and said, "Your boss told me."

"What?" Caleb looked shocked. "He wouldn't do that. Why would he do that?"

"Why do you think?" Clint asked. "Why do you think he had you kill Larry?"

"He couldn't trust Larry," Caleb said, not bothering to deny it.

"So after you and Larry beat Harry Hayes to death, he had you get rid of Larry."

"It was Larry who beat the old man to death," Caleb said. "I couldn't stop him."

"Well, I guess your boss is just playing the odds," Clint said. "Makes more sense to him to have me kill you."

"He hired you to kill me?"

"No, but he figured if I found you here, you'd be dumb enough to go for your gun."

"I ain't as dumb as he thinks," Caleb said. "I wouldn't never slap leather with you."

"Then *you* are smarter than he thinks," Clint said. "Let's see how smart you really are." Clint sat himself down on a hay bale, across from Caleb.

"Whataya want?" Caleb asked.

"I got part of what I want," Clint said. "Teach sent you and Larry out to kill Harry Hayes, right?"

"He sent us to shut 'im up," Caleb said. "Larry took it too far."

Clint thought it was an easy thing for Caleb to blame the dead man. But his reply still incriminated Hiram Teach.

"Look," Caleb said, "I'm done in Firecreek. I just wanna leave. So tell me what I gotta do."

"Okay," Clint said, "here it is . . ."

# Chapter Thirty-Nine

"Teach has a handful of guns he uses when he has to," Caleb said. "They're expensive. He has to get some of the other council members in town to foot the bill."

"Does that usually include Race Gentry?"

"How'd you know that?"

"A hunch."

"Okay," Clint said, "I still want you to tell him what I told you."

"Then I can go? I can leave town?"

"I'll tell you when."

"When do you want me to tell 'im?"

"Today."

"Then what?"

"Then do what you've been doing," Clint said. "Stay out of sight. But make sure I know where you are."

"All right."

They both stood up.

"Caleb, if you leave town before I tell you to, I'll hunt you down. Understand?"

"Sure, I understand. but where should I stay?"

"Where do you live?"

"A shack outside of town."

"Then I'll find you there. Now go on, you get out of here first."

"My gun?"

"Pick it up, carefully," Clint said.

"Don't worry," Caleb said. "I wouldn't try nothin' with you." He picked up the gun and holstered it. "My knife?"

"I don't like what you did with that knife," Clint said. "Leave it."

"My ol' pappy gave it to—"

"Leave it!"

"Yessir," Caleb said, and left the barn.

Clint sat back down on the hay bale. He was pretty sure he had Teach now, but the man probably had time to send for his top guns. With any luck Clint would know at least one of them and be able to talk to him.

Rather than return to his hotel, Clint simply doused the lamp and went back to his hay bed.

***

When Clint did return to his hotel the next morning, the desk clerk looked away. This caused Clint to believe that someone was in his room. When he got to his door, he pressed his ear to it. Hearing nothing, he drew his gun, unlocked the door and slammed it open. He darted into the room with his gun held out ahead of him.

The woman in the bed screamed.

"You scared the shit out of me!" Alma shouted, holding the sheet in front of her.

Clint slammed the door and holstered his gun.

"What are you doing here?" he asked.

"I came looking for you this morning, after my bath," she said. "You weren't here, so I thought I'd wait. I fell asleep."

"Naked?"

She smiled.

"Why not?"

Clint walked past her to hang his gunbelt on the bedpost. This afforded her a look at his back.

"You have hay on your back," she said. "You been rollin' around in the hay with some young thing?"

"No," he said. "I slept in a barn."

"Why'd you do that when you have a hotel room?"

"It's a long story."

He sat in a chair to remove his boots. She leapt off the bed, and got to her knees in front of him to help.

"Thanks," he said, sitting back.

"You look pretty exhausted for someone who slept in a barn," she said.

"I am," he said. "I was going to get a couple of hours here."

She got to her feet and jumped on the bed.

"Then come on," she said.

"You think my getting into bed with you is going to get me some rest?"

"Why not?"

"Not with that body."

"I'll just cradle you," she promised, "to my bosom."

"Not a chance."

She laughed, transforming her tired face into something pretty.

"You should smile more," he told her.

"Not much to smile about."

"Okay," he said, starting to undress, "why are you here?"

"To warn you."

"About what?"

"Teach is up to something," she said.

"How do you know?"

"Because last night he fucked me like a whore, rolled off and left me alone. This morning he went out early to send some telegrams."

"I was afraid of that," Clint said. "He's sending for help."

"That's what I thought," she said.

"But why warn me?" he asked. "You're his woman."

"I'm the woman he uses," she said. "That could change at any time. You gave me more consideration as a woman in one night than he has ever done. Is that good enough for you?"

"It'll have to be. You have to get dressed and go."

She got to her knees on the bed and ran her hands down her bountiful body, then back up to cup her breasts and thumb her nipples.

"Are you sure?"

"Damn you!" he swore and grabbed her.

# Chapter Forty

After Alma left, he saw that there was no point in going to sleep. He decided to try and find out just who Hiram Teach had sent telegrams to. That meant using the sheriff. He used the pitcher-and-basin in the room to clean up, got dressed, strapped on his gun and left.

Down in the lobby he stopped at the front desk.

"Yes, Sir?"

"If you ever let anyone else into my room while I'm out, I'll be very unhappy. You understand?"

"Oh, y-yessir," he said, "but Alma—"

"I know," Clint said. "She's very convincing. But don't let it happen again. Understand?"

"Uh, no Sir—I mean, yessir."

Clint left the hotel.

***

Clint found Harlow leaving his office, locking the door behind him.

"Where are you off to?" Clint asked.

"Breakfast," Harlow said. "I spent the night in my office. I thought it would be safer."

"I'll have breakfast with you," Clint said, "but let's stop at the telegraph office."

"What for?"

"I understand Teach sent some telegrams out," Clint said. "I want to see who he sent them to."

"Why?"

"I think he's sending for some more guns."

They started walking together.

"Is this a hunch?"

"No," Clint said, "I was warned."

"By who?"

"Alma," Clint said, "and Caleb."

Harlow stopped walking.

"You found him?"

"Yes," Clint said. "He came to the livery to collect his horse. Teach told him to leave town."

"And?"

"I convinced him not to."

"And apparently you convinced him to talk."

"Yes."

"What'd he say?"

"I'll tell you at breakfast."

They started walking again.

"Why don't you go to the telegraph office your-self?" Harlow asked.

"The clerk might refuse to tell me what I want to know," Clint said. "But you're wearing a badge."

"I see."

When they got to the telegraph office, Clint decided to stay outside.

"We just need to know who they went to," he told Harlow, "not what they said."

"Right."

Harlow went inside and came out in about ten minutes.

"Got them?" Clint asked.

"Yes."

"What are they?"

"I'll tell you at breakfast."

***

Harlow took Clint to a small café he hadn't been to before.

"What are the names?" Clint asked, after they had ordered.

Harlow pushed a slip of paper across the table to Clint.

"Do you know them?" the lawman asked.

"I've heard of all of them," Clint said. "They're top guns."

"Do you know any of them, personally?"

"One," Clint said, putting the slip of paper into his pocket.

"Which one?"

"Dallas Bogard."

"Not Dan?" Harlow asked.

"No," Clint said, "Dan's in prison for killing a law-man."

"Is this his brother?"

"Nobody knows," Clint said, "but he's a fast man with a gun."

"And the other two?"

"I don't know them personally, but I've heard of them."

"Are they good?"

"Very."

"What's gonna happen if you have to face the three of them at once?"

"I'll probably end up dead."

"So are you gonna leave town?"

"No."

"But—"

"If I leave town, the word will get out that I ran from a fight," Clint said. "I'd be dead within weeks anyway."

"So whatta are you gonna do?"

"Well, if we can put Teach away before they get here, he won't be able to pay them, and I won't have to worry."

"And if we can't put him away?"

"I may be able to talk to Bogard," Clint said.

"And get him not to take the job?"

Clint nodded.

"And maybe get him to back me."

"Are you that friendly with him?"

"Not particularly," Clint said, "but Dallas has his own code of ethics."

"And what are they?"

"One of them is, he never turns down an interesting job," Clint said.

"Sounds like you're in trouble," Harlow said. "What else?"

"One other one I can think of," Clint said.

"What's that?"

"He never gangs up on one man."

# Chapter Forty-One

"What did Caleb have to say?" Harlow asked.

"He pretty much confirmed what we thought. Oh, he says Teach told them to shut Harry up, and that Larry got carried away and beat the old man to death."

"Blamin' it on a dead man," Harlow said.

"Right."

"Then I can't prove it," Harlow said. "I can't arrest Caleb or Teach. Did Caleb admit to killin' Larry?"

"No," Clint said, "but he didn't deny it."

"Then I can't arrest him."

"You will, soon," Clint said, "him and Teach."

"If you don't mind me askin'," Harlow said, "why don't you just kill 'em both and be done with it?"

"Like you said," Clint answered, "there's no proof. And I'm not a killer, Sheriff, no matter what you think, or what you've heard."

"Sorry," Harlow said, "I didn't mean—"

"Yeah, you did," Clint said, "but that's all right. I'm used to it."

They finished their breakfast and left the café.

"What's Caleb doin' now?" Harlow asked.

"Staying out of sight until I say so."

"And when will that be?"

"I assume there's a judge in town," Clint said.

"Yes, Judge Dodd."

"If you make an arrest, will he back you?"

"He doesn't think much of me," Harlow admitted.

"But you *are* the law," Clint said.

"If I arrest Caleb, maybe," Harlow said, "but I don't know about Teach."

"We'll have to see when the time comes," Clint said. "Meanwhile, you might as well go back to your office."

"And you?"

"I'm going to have another talk with Teach," Clint said.

"You gonna tell 'im you know about his guns?" Harlow asked.

"I don't know what I'm going to tell him," Clint said. "I might just wave Caleb in his face."

"What do you think he'll do?"

"Nothing until his guns get here."

"I can tell you one thing."

"What's that?"

"He's not gonna want to foot the bill for those guns, himself. He'll try and get some of the other council members to put up some money."

"Will they?"

Harlow shrugged.

"Who knows? Several of them are completely under Teach's thumb. Some of the others have minds of their own."

"Then we'll just have to see, won't we?"

"Have you given any more thought to ridin' out?"

"No," Clint said, "that's still out of the question."

"You're a stubborn man, Mr. Adams."

"I'm often stubborn, Sheriff," Clint said, "and sometimes foolish, but I feel I owe something to Harry Hayes, who I believe died for no reason."

"You're probably right about that," Harlow said.

"I'll let you know when I think we need to talk to Judge Dodd."

"I'll be waitin' in my office."

The two men split up and went their own ways . . .

***

When Clint entered the Full House Saloon, it was in full swing. He looked at the bartender across the room and pointed to the back. The bartender nodded, indicating that Teach was in his office.

Clint entered without knocking.

"You again?"

"I just thought I'd tell you I found Caleb," Clint said.

"And you killed him? That's too bad."

"I didn't kill him."

"Then what did you do?"

"I tucked him away somewhere until he can talk to Sheriff Harlow and Judge Dodd."

"Talk about what?"

"You."

"I don't know what you think Caleb can tell you about me, Adams."

"I guess we'll find out, won't we?" Clint said.

"Why don't you just get out of my office?" Teach said.

"I'll do that," Clint said, "but I'll be back,"

"I look forward to it."

Clint left the office, having given Teach something to think about.

\*\*\*

After leaving the Full House Saloon, Clint had second thoughts about leaving Caleb at his shack. He decided to go out there and fetch him and stash him in the hotel.

\*\*\*

Teach wished he had someone to send after Caleb now, but he didn't, not until Dallas Bogard and the other guns got to town. Bogard was a big enough name to take care of Clint Adams. The other two could deal with Caleb. If Adams brought Harlow and Judge Dodd into the matter, he would have to deal with them.

He had a gun in his top drawer. He wished he had the guts to pull it out and shoot Adams. But he knew he didn't.

He had met with some of the members of the Town Council and got them to agree to put up some money. They didn't know exactly what for, but then, they didn't want to know. He wished he could have managed to get Race Gentry involved, but the owner of the Jack of Spades Saloon was starting to develop a mind of his own. He might turn out to be a problem, but first Teach would have to deal with Ben Clifford.

It would all turn out all right once the Gunsmith was gone. Bogard and the other two gunmen would be there in two days. He just had to stay in control until they arrived, and then they would take care of Clint Adams and he would be free to take care of the rest.

# Chapter Forty-Two

Clint stuck Caleb in a room down the hall from his and told him not to leave.

"What if I get hungry?"

"I'll bring you some food."

"What about Mr. Teach's hired guns?"

"I'll take care of them."

"Yeah, what if they take care of you?" Caleb asked.

"Then you and your boss can go back to business as usual," Clint said.

"I dunno if I wanna do that," Caleb said.

"Then, if they kill me, you better get out of town fast."

***

Clint decided to go back to sitting outside the hotel until Teach's guns rode in. That way he could also make sure nothing happened to Caleb. The only way to get Teach was if Caleb talked to Judge Dodd. For that to happen, Harlow would have to arrest him.

But before the arrest, Clint decided he should talk to Judge Dodd himself, and he had to do it alone, without

Sheriff Harlow. For that he would try City Hall first, to see if the Judge had an office there.

\*\*\*

He found a man in City Hall sweeping the floors.

"Naw, Judge Dodd ain't got an office here," the man told him. "It's down the street some. Got a shingle outside."

"Thanks." He started away, then turned back. "Didn't this used to be Harry Hayes' job?"

"Sure was, but now that he's dead I gotta do it."

Clint left City Hall and walked down the street. He found the shingle with JUDGE MALCOM DODD written on it.

As he entered, he saw an older man in a black three-piece suit, sitting behind a desk and pouring himself a whiskey.

"Just a second, young fella," the man said. "Medicinal purposes, you understand." He tossed off the whiskey and put the bottle back in the desk. "Now what can I do for you?"

"My name's Clint Adams. Are you Judge Dodd?"

"I am, indeed," the Judge said. "Say, ain't you the Gunsmith?"

"I am."

"I heard you were in town."

"What else did you hear?"

"That you're lookin' for trouble."

"That's not exactly right, Judge," Clint said. "But I am looking for the men who killed Harry Hayes."

"Poor Harry," Dodd said. "I knew him a long time."

"Then you have an interest in who killed him," Clint said, "as an officer of the court and a friend."

"Well, yes . . ."

"So if Sheriff Harlow can make an arrest, you'll prosecute?"

"Well," Dodd said, "if he has proof."

"And it doesn't matter who it is?"

Dodd's eyes narrowed.

"What are you gettin' at, Mr. Adams?"

"I have proof that Hiram Teach was behind Harry's death. Also, the death of a young man named Larry, who Teach had kill Harry."

"This sounds very confusing," the judge said. "I think I need another drink—" As he started to open his desk drawer Clint stepped forward and stopped him.

"I need you sober, Judge," Clint said. "I'm going to help Sheriff Harlow bring in Hiram Teach and you're going to put him on trial."

"Teach is an important man in this town."

"So important he can get away with murder?"

"Well . . . no, but . . . how do you intend to prove it?"

"One of his men is willing to testify that Teach sent him and Larry after Harry Hayes. I also have word that Teach is bringing in three gunmen to take care of me."

"Jesus," Dodd said. "What if they kill you?"

"Then you can forget the whole thing," Clint said, "but I'm going to try to get one of those men to testify that Hiram Teach hired him to kill me."

"This all sounds very iffy, Mr. Adams," Judge Dodd said.

"I agree," Clint said, "but I'm going to make it all happen. I just need you to back the sheriff's play when he makes the arrests. Can you do that, Judge?"

"I . . . well, I . . ." The man cleared his throat. "If you have proof of all this, I'll sit on the bench."

"Good," Clint stood up straight. "This might take a few days for those gunmen to get here. Go ahead and have your medicinal sips, but for Godssake, stay sober."

"Yeeh, yes," Judge Dodd said, "of course"

Clint left the judge's office, hoping against hope that the older judge would be able to keep his sips medicinal.

# Chapter Forty-Three

Clint did, indeed, feel foolish, but there was nothing else to do now but wait for Teach's gunmen to arrive. He took up his former position in front of the hotel to watch for the arrival of the three gunmen. What he didn't know was that follow up telegrams had been sent, telling the men not to ride down main street, but to ride to Teach's Freight and Stage Station.

They arrived on the same day, but separately. The last to arrive was Dallas Bogard.

As he entered the freight station, Hiram Teach shook the gunman's hand.

"Glad to see you, Bogard," Teach said. "The other two are here."

"Who are they?" Bogard asked.

"Anse Granger and Bill Philips."

"I don't know them."

"They're not as well known as you" Teach said, "but they're fast. Come on, I'll introduce you."

They passed through the front sitting room of the building into the back office, where Granger and Philips were waiting.

"Boys," Teach said "this is Dallas Bogard."

Bogard was older than the other two. The two younger men stood up and eyed Bogard warily. Granger wore a gun on his left side, while Philips wore two. Bogard had a Peacemaker on his right hip.

"Gladda meet ya," Granger said.

Philips simply nodded.

"Now that you're all here, you're probably wondering why I sent for you."

"It must be a big job, for you to hire all three of us," Granger said.

"It is," Teach said, "the biggest."

"Well," Bogard said, "don't keep us waiting."

"It's Clint Adams," Teach said. "I want you to kill the Gunsmith."

"He's here, in town?" Granger asked.

"He is, and he's in my way," Teach said.

"When do you want it done?" Philips asked.

"Right away," Teach said, "today. The fool is sitting out in front of his hotel, waiting."

"Waiting for what?" Granger asked.

"For you," Teach said.

"He knows we're comin'?" Philips asked.

"He knows somebody's coming," Teach said. "He doesn't know who."

"You want the three of us to gun down Adams," Bogard said.

"That's right," Teach said. "He'll never stand up to the three of you."

Bogard didn't like the idea of three against one, especially when the one was the Gunsmith. He knew and respected the man. Gunning down Clint Adams didn't bother him, but doing it three to one did.

"I want to get a room and clean up," Bogard said.

The others looked at him.

"I guess that don't sound so bad," Granger said. "I rode a long way. A meal would be nice."

"Yeah," Philips said, "I'm kinda hungry."

"You can eat after the job," Teach said.

"Rushing into something like this ain't a good idea," Bogard said. "You boys should know that."

Granger and Philips exchanged a look, then Granger said, "Well, yeah, of course we know that."

"I don't understand this," Teach said. "I want it done quick."

Bogard looked at Teach.

"I don't know about these boys, but you can hire me to do a job, but you can't tell me where and when to do it. That's a sure way for me to get killed. Now, where can I get a room?"

# Chapter Forty-Four

Since Bogard and the others wanted rooms, Teach told them to ride to the Full House Saloon, and he'd give them rooms upstairs. But he had them ride down Main Street after all, right past Clint Adams' hotel.

"That him?" Granger asked.

"That's him," Bogard said.

"He don't look like much," Philips said.

"Don't be a fool," Bogard said.

"You know 'im?" Granger said.

Bogard nodded and said, "I know 'im."

\*\*\*

Clint saw the three gunmen riding past him, Bogard in the lead. He figured they were riding to Teach's saloon. His options were to stay where he was and wait, or go over to the Full House and press the issue. He decided that since he had been waiting for most of his time in Firecreek, it wouldn't hurt to wait a bit longer and see how Bogard and the others wanted to play it.

\*\*\*

Teach showed the three men to their rooms, complete with water to clean up with. He told them to meet him in the saloon in two hours. As soon as he was gone, Bogard decided to take a walk.

***

When Clint saw Bogard walking up the street toward him, he knew he had made the right decision.

"Adams," Bogard said.

"Hello, Dallas," Clint said. "Have a seat."

Bogard got a chair and pulled it over.

"What's this all about?" he asked, seating himself. "Why have three men been hired to kill you?"

"Hiram Teach is trying to make sure I don't get him arrested."

"For what?"

"Murder."

"Did he do it himself?"

"He hired it done," Clint said. "Then had the man who did it killed. I have the man who killed him hidden away. He's going to testify."

"And if we kill you?"

"Then he won't testify."

"This doesn't sound like a very good deal for you, Adams. Why are you involved?"

"Believe it or not, I started out just minding my own business," Clint said. "Then I met a man, and a girl—"

"There's always a girl," Bogard said.

"Seems like it," Clint said. "And the girl has a father who's opposing the sitting mayor. Look, it has to do with the railroad coming through, only Teach doesn't seem to like that idea. I'm in Teach's way and I want to put him in jail. It's as simple as that. And then I'm gone."

"Or dead."

"Now you've got it. And making me dead is your job, unless I can talk you out of it."

"You've still got two more guns to deal with."

"Who are they? Anybody you know?"

"Never heard of them," Bogard said. "Their names are Granger and Philips."

"I don't know them, either. So you don't know if they're any good?"

"They're about thirty, so I guess they've stayed alive this long."

"What about you, Dallas?" Clint asked.

"I'm here to do a job," Bogard said. "And it's gonna pay well."

"So you're going to do it?"

"I don't like the odds," Bogard said. "If I stand against you, it'll be one-on-one, so I tell you what. I'll let the other two have a try first. Then, if you kill them, you'll have to deal with me."

"If you leave me to them, it sounds like you're giving up your payday anyway."

"Somehow, I don't think that's gonna happen," Bogard said. "I've seen you in action."

"Why not just ride out?" Clint asked.

"I could ask you the same question," Bogard said.

"Touche," Clint said. "I'm committed."

"When I take a job, I'm also committed. I can't just ride out."

"Dallas—"

"Sorry, Clint," Bogard said, standing, "that's the best I can do."

"Then I guess the best man will win," Clint said.

"I've always wondered," Bogard said. "This way, we'll find out."

"When will you all be coming?" Clint asked.

"After a meal."

"Okay, then," Clint said, "I'll be right here."

Bogard started away, then turned back.

"I'll make sure nobody bushwhacks you."

"I appreciate it."

As Bogard walked away Clint reviewed the conversation. Bogard was one of the fastest guns he had ever seen. This would be interesting, for sure.

# Chapter Forty-Five

Alma served the three gunmen their meals, paid for by Teach.

"Our next meal should hopefully be better than this," Granger said.

"If there is a next meal," Bogard said.

"There's three of us and one of him," Philips said. "You think there's gonna be a problem?"

"We're talkin' about Clint Adams," Bogard said. "For at least one of you, this is your last meal."

"And what if it's your last meal?" Granger asked.

"Every meal could be my last," Bogard said. "It's the nature of the business."

Granger and Philips exchanged a look.

"I don't like this kind of talk," Philips said. "Maybe we oughtta just bushwhack him."

"I'm not a bushwhacker," Bogard said. "I face men full on. If you wanna backshoot Adams, you'll do it without me."

"What the hell," Granger said. "We all still get paid once he's dead, right?"

"Just let me know how you two wanna play it," Bogard told them.

Granger and Philips exchanged another look.

"Okay, we'll do it your way," Granger said. "Face-to-face. Do you know where Adams is?"

"I do."

"I had a feeling you went to see him when you went for a walk."

"Did you warn him?" Philips asked.

"There was no need," Bogard said. "He knows we're comin'."

***

The three gunmen left the café and walked toward Clint's hotel. He saw them coming and knew it was time. Hopefully, after this, it would all be over, and he would still be standing. But it depended on whether or not Bogard stuck to what he said he would do. If the man stood with the other two, Clint knew he would have to kill Bogard first.

"You boys have a good meal?" he asked, as they stopped in front of him.

"It was terrible," Granger said.

"If you're still standing after this, have your boss take you to the Cattleman's Steak House. The food is great."

"Yeah, we'll do that, Adams," Philips said.

Clint stood and asked, "Are you ready for this? You have time to change your minds, you know."

"We ain't gonna change our minds, are we, boys?" Granger said.

"That's not exactly true," Bogard said.

The other two men looked at him.

"Whataya mean?" Granger asked.

"I don't like three-to-one odds," Bogard said, "so I'm gonna leave Adams to you two."

"Hey," Granger said, "you got a job to do."

"If he kills the two of you," Bogard said, "I'll do my job. But for now . . . have at it."

He moved aside, out of the line of fire, to watch.

"There you go, boys," Clint said. "Now you have one more chance to change your minds."

But they weren't about to do that. He saw it in their demeanor. They both went for their guns, and Clint could see they were two-bit gunmen. He drew and fired twice, knocking both men off their feet and onto their backs.

Bogard moved in, bent and checked both men.

"Dead center, both of 'em," he said.

Clint ejected the spent shells and loaded live ones, then holstered his gun.

"Where does that leave us, Dallas?" Clint asked.

Bogard turned to face Clint, wiped the back of his left hand across his mouth.

"Whata you need, Clint?" he asked.

"I need you to testify that Teach hired you and these two boys to gun me down."

"Instead of drawin' on you right now," Bogard said.

"That's right."

"Well," Bogard said, "you were pretty fast. You ain't lost a lick, have you?"

"I hope not," Clint said. "I don't want to draw on you to find out, Dallas. I also don't want to kill you. Not for a tinhorn like Hiram Teach."

"Yeah," Bogard said, "I didn't spend much time with him, but I sure didn't like 'im."

"And me?"

"Well," Bogard said, "I like you fine, Clint. I think in a couple or three more years, I could probably take you."

"Not now?"

Bogard pushed his hat back on his head and said, "Right now I'll testify for ya."

"I appreciate that, Dallas," Clint said. "I'm looking to put this town behind me, and I'm hoping not to get myself into any more messes like this one."

"You think that's possible?"

"I think I'm going to give it a good, decent try." People started to gather around them. "Let's go and see the sheriff."

# Chapter Forty-Six

Two days later, Clint walked into Holly's dress shop, the bell tinkling his arrival. She looked up from her counter and smiled.

"Is it over?" she asked.

"It's over," Clint said. "Judge Dodd found Teach guilty and sentenced him to the territorial state prison."

"And his men?"

"They pretty much scattered when he was arrested, Caleb testified, but the Judge sentenced him, as well."

"Is that fair?"

"Well, he was in on the killing of Harry Hayes, and he killed his own partner. He's got to pay for that."

"Did you tell my father?"

"He was in the courtroom."

"So what will happen now?"

"When the time comes, your father will run for mayor. He'll probably beat Big Bill."

"And then things around here will change," she said.

"Without Hiram Teach around, I'd say so. The railroad will probably come in. That'll cause big changes."

She came around the counter to face him.

"I can't thank you enough, Clint," she said. "What will you do now?"

"I'll ride out and do my best to mind my own business from now on."

She laughed.

"I doubt that you can do that," she said. "Not the kind of man you are." She kissed him on the cheek and said, "Take care."

"You, too."

He turned and left the store. His horse was tied out front, so he mounted the Tobiano and turned him in time to see Dallas Bogard riding toward him.

"Leavin' town?" Bogard asked.

"I am," Clint said. "Thanks for your help, Dallas."

"Like I said in the beginnin'," Bogard said, "I didn't like the odds."

"Where are you off to?" Clint asked.

"I dunno," Bogard said. "Lookin' for another job, I guess."

"You want to ride together?" Clint asked.

"A ways," Bogard said. "I pretty much like ridin' on my own."

"So do I," Clint said, "but I don't see the harm in riding together for a spell."

"A short spell," Bogard said.

Clint smiled and said, "Agreed."

*Upcoming New Release!*

# THE GUNSMITH

## THE GUNSMITH DOWN UNDER
### BOOK 488

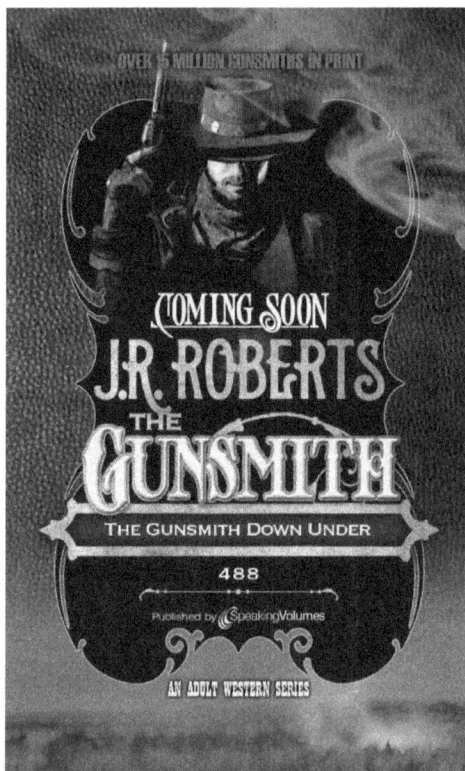

For more information
visit: www.SpeakingVolumes.us

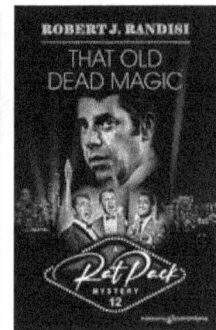

*Now Available!*

# THE GUNSMITH GIANT SERIES

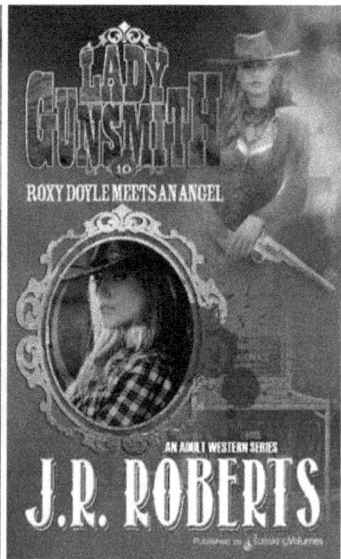

# Now Available!

## AWARD-WINNING AUTHOR
## ROBERT J. RANDISI (J.R. ROBERTS)

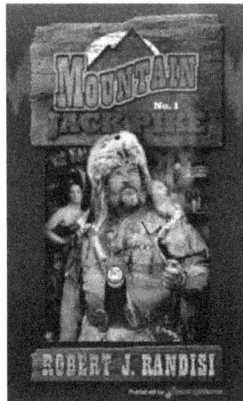

**For more information**
**visit:** www.SpeakingVolumes.us

*Now Available!*

**AWARD-WINNING AUTHOR
ROBERT J. RANDISI
TALBOT ROPER NOVELS**

**For more information
visit: www.SpeakingVolumes.us**